Surfing For Love

Shore Thing Series

Bree Kraemer

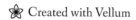

Chapter One

Penny

Was there anything better than spending time at a beach with your best friends where someone brought you unlimited drinks?

If there was, Penny didn't know about it.

She was already halfway through her five days of bliss and was wishing they'd opted to stay longer. The real world was fine, but it didn't compare to laughing with her friends in the sun.

Jodi, always the pragmatic one, had insisted that five days was enough. She was never letting Jodi make decisions again.

They came on this trip to celebrate turning twenty-five. While not all of their birthdays were in the same month, or even technically in the same year, they met in college and became fast friends. When they graduated, they'd made the decision to once a year get away from it all and do something fun. Typically, it was a weekend, and they stayed close to home doing things like shopping, trying out new restaurants, or even going to concerts.

They'd wanted something big for the big two-five.

They all realized that twenty-five wasn't old, but to them, it sort of felt like a big milestone in their lives; one they wanted to celebrate.

So they'd come up with dates that worked for all of them, handed the planning over to Jodi, and let her do her thing.

Turns out, her thing had been five days at an all inclusive resort in Cancun.

This was paradise to Penny.

She'd never been to Cancun or even out of the country before. In fact, she'd only ever been to a beach once in her life, and that was her freshman year of college, during Spring Break in Florida. Where, if she thought back, she wasn't sure she'd spent more than a few hours in the sun.

Most of that trip was spent drunk, hooking up with a guy named Antonio, or passed out in her room.

Not the best image of herself.

Her mom would be appalled if she knew the things she'd gotten into during college, which was why she kept that info to herself. Or, at least between herself and her friends.

Jodi, Mya, and Annabelle had all been on that trip, and all of them except Annabelle had basically the same Spring Break experience.

At the time, Annabelle had a boyfriend, so she'd refrained from hooking up with anyone and instead used the time to work on her tan and ensure the rest of them stayed safe.

Momma Annabelle, as they liked to call her.

Oddly enough, since breaking up with that guy a few

months later, Annabelle had been the one who needed to be looked after.

She'd gone sort of wild springbreaker for about a year.

"You know," Mya said, her voice carrying from the last lounge chair where she was sitting, because quiet was not a word she knew, "I think we should do a beach trip every year."

"Seconded," Annabelle said from right beside Penny as she raised her drink in the air.

"You guys say that now," Jodi said. "But when I go to plan it, you'll all have excuses for why you can't come."

"Now that I've been here, I will never have an excuse not to come back," Penny said, waving a hand in the air. "Plan away, and count me in!"

"Why is it so busy all of a sudden?" Annabelle asked.

Penny looked around and noticed Annabelle was right. The pool had double the amount of people as the previous two days. Looking closer, she noticed most of those people were men.

"There was a tech retreat that apparently ended yesterday," Jodi said, as if she knew everything all the time. Which she usually did.

"How in the hell do you know that?" Penny asked.

"The bartender told me." She said it as if it was a foregone conclusion that the bartender should tell her everything. Again, it usually was.

"Oh, more guys to ogle," Mya said, sitting up straight and looking out toward the pool.

"Did you not hear her say tech retreat?" Penny said. "These are not guys you ogle. Marry, probably, but for their personality, not for their looks."

"Excuse me," Annabelle said. "I work in tech, and I think I am ogleable."

"One," Jodi said. "That's not a word, and two, you're the exception, not the rule."

"There are hot guys at my office." Annabelle sounded offended.

"Rhys doesn't count as a tech guy. He's a project manager." Penny couldn't see Mya's eyes, but she knew they were rolling behind her sunglasses.

"Rhys has a hot guy name and the face to match," Jodi said wistfully.

"He's also fucking annoying," Annabelle said. "So, while hot on the outside, he's ugly on the inside."

"It's not his insides I want to see while he fucks me," Jodi said.

Penny laughed, sitting back and listening to her friends bicker while she took in the guys who had congregated at the pool for the day. They were of all ages and races, but they all had one thing in common: they looked like what they were. Tech guys.

She knew it was a stereotype, and sometimes she hated herself for falling into that trap. She would hate it if someone did the same to her, which they often did. They used her name as a way to say things like "Penny is a little girl's name" or "I'm not sure I can trust advice on my finances from someone named Penny". They also assumed that because she was a woman, she wasn't great at her job.

All of that sucked because she was fucking amazing at her job. Finance was definitely a man's world, but like tech, more and more women were joining the field. And like her, more often than not, most had a head for numbers and could outthink the men they worked with.

It was just going to take time to make people and the world accept that.

Part of that would be to stop with the stereotypes. Something she needed to do herself when it came to tech guys. "You know what, I'm going to go mingle."

"Me too!" Annabelle jumped up to join her.

Together, they took their drinks and waded into the pool.

"There really are a lot of them," Annabelle said.

"Must have been a big retreat. I wonder what company it is?" As they moved through the water, they smiled at a few people.

"We should have asked Jodi, I'm sure she got that info from the bartender."

They both laughed as they passed a group of five guys.

"Hey," one said. "How's it going?"

Not shy. That was a point in his favor. "Good. How are you?"

"Better now that I'm not working." He held out his hand. "I'm Joe."

"Hi Joe, I'm Penny, and this is my friend Annabelle." They all shook hands.

Another guy stepped forward. "And I'm Matt." Penny shook his hand too.

Neither one was what you'd call hot, but they were both cute and obviously friendly. That was important. "What sort of work were you here for?" she asked, playing dumb since she already knew.

"It was a company retreat," Matt answered first.

"What do you guys do?" Annabelle asked.

"We're in IT," Joe said.

"Cool," Annabelle said, as if it were a big deal. "I'm in IT too."

5

"Oh yeah," Matt said like it was amazing, but then ruined it. "Let me guess, a business analyst?"

Next to her, Penny felt Annabelle stiffen. "No," she said sternly, and her voice let Penny know that Matt was toast. "I'm a developer."

The idiot Matt had the nerve to laugh. At least Joe cringed and gave Penny a look that clearly said, 'I'm sorry for my sexist friend'. "I'm sure you are," Matt said.

"What's that supposed to mean?" Annabelle shouted. So loudly that several people nearby turned to look in their direction.

Joe grabbed Matt's arm. "We'll leave you alone," he said, pulling his friend away.

"What an ass," Annabelle said. "How dare he insinuate that I'm not a developer? He did everything but add the 'honey' onto the end of his words."

"Not everyone thinks like that."

"But the ones who do ruin it for everyone."

They started walking again, and as they moved through the pool, Penny looked up, her eyes landing on two guys standing far back from the pool. She couldn't be sure, but it looked as if both of them were looking in their direction. Both were in swim trunks, and both had bodies that looked as if they spent at least a little time in the gym—not big muscles, but lean. These were most likely not tech guys.

The one she couldn't seem to take her eyes off of was holding a surfboard.

And he looked damn fine standing there holding it.

"Now, there are guys I wouldn't mind ogling," Annabelle said wistfully.

Thank God for sunglasses, so she could look her fill

without him ever knowing—at least, she hoped. He continued to stare in her direction, making her a little self-conscious, but not enough to stop her from staring at him.

Should she talk to him? Maybe she could turn a conversation into more. More being sex. He made her body tingle with sexual energy, and while she'd sworn to herself that she wouldn't have sex with a random guy on this trip, this guy made her consider amending that thought.

If there was ever a time to have sex with a stranger, it was with one who looked like he did.

Decision made, she looked at Annabelle. "Let's go talk to them."

Annabelle tilted her head and pursed her lips. "That's going to be a problem since they're gone."

"What?" Penny whipped her head around, and sure enough, the spot they'd been standing in was now empty. "Where'd they go?" She scanned the surrounding areas, coming up empty.

"How should I know? It doesn't matter anyway. Did you or did you not say you weren't hooking up with anyone on this trip?" Even with her sunglasses on, Penny could see Annabelle's raised eyebrows.

"A woman can change her mind."

Annabelle laughed. "She definitely can." She twined her arm through Penny's. "Let's get another drink and talk about how ridiculously hot those guys were. Because let me tell you, the one on the left was so hot that I won't need porn for the foreseeable future."

Penny knew just what she was talking about. The vision of the surfboard guy would keep her warm for many nights to come.

They each ordered another drink at the bar before sitting on the stools in the water. Cancun really was her version of heaven. Where else could you sit on a stool in the water and drink as much as you wanted?

"Which one were you looking at?" Annabelle asked. "Surfboard guy or brooding, angry guy?"

"Since I had no idea there was a brooding, angry guy, I think you have your answer." She'd barely taken her eyes off the surfboard guy to notice the guy next to him.

"Oh yeah, he looked like he wanted to strangle someone, and fuck if it wasn't hot." She fanned her face. "Seriously. Why are bad boys so hot? Why can't nice, sweet guys be hot?"

"You have no clue if he's a bad boy." Even as she said it, she was sure that both the brooding guy and the surfboard guy had a little bit of bad boy inside them.

She scoffed. "If you'd taken your eyes off surfboard guy for one second, you would have noticed that steam was practically coming out of my guy's ears. Maybe he knows asshole Matt and wanted to come to my rescue."

Annabelle had a knight in shining armor complex if there ever was one. "Your guy?" Penny lowered her sunglasses from her eyes, her eyes wide as she looked at her friend. "I see your delusions have already taken over."

"Fuck you," Annabelle said with no real passion. "They're dreams, not delusions. There's a difference."

"Sure there is." She put her sunglasses back into place. "Anyway, it doesn't matter. They're gone and we're probably better off for it. No matter how hot, it's not like anything can come from one night of sex."

"Orgasms. Very good orgasms can come from a night of sex." Annabelle plucked the orange from her drink, sucking on it. "God, I need an orgasm. Do you know how long it's been since I've had one that I haven't given myself?" She didn't wait for Penny to answer. "Eight months. Eight long, tortuous months."

"You make it seem like eight months is a long time." She was going on close to a year, and like Annabelle, she was starting to get the itch for more than her fingers or a toy.

"It is!" She slammed her hand down on the bar. "I've never gone eight months without sex. Not since I started having it. I was addicted from day one."

That was the truth. Annabelle was one of those people who went from guy to guy, relationship to relationship, like it was no big deal. She was always looking for Mister Right and he hadn't shown up yet.

But, dreamer that she was, she kept putting herself out there and trying.

Penny wished she could be more like her. But, sometimes it was nice to be alone. She liked her space and her schedule. When she was in a relationship, guys just got in the way. Her mom said that was a true sign she hadn't met Mister Right yet. Apparently, when the right person came along, she'd be cool sharing her space and having a fucked up calendar.

Every time her mom mentioned it, she held back an eye roll.

Why did she have to change? Why couldn't the guy learn to give her space and respect her schedule?

"What are you two bitches doing over here?" Jodi's voice had her turning her head to find both Jodi and Mya right behind them in the water.

"Daydreaming about hot guys who look like they could give us amazing orgasms," Annabelle answered.

"Well, that is the dream," Mya said, taking the empty stool next to Penny.

"What happened in the pool?" Jodi asked. "I saw you talking to a couple of guys and then saw Annabelle go all feral and thought we were going to have to bail her out of a Mexican jail."

"I did not get feral, but, for your information, he was condescending, and when I mentioned I was a developer, he basically patted me on the head and said, 'That's cute, honey.'" Annabelle mimicked the gesture by patting Mya on the head.

"HE DIDN'T!?" Mya said in outrage, reaching to the side and stealing Penny's drink, taking a huge sip.

"For that, I would have bailed you out of jail," Jodi said.

"If the nerdy guys are becoming jerks, we can kiss amazing orgasms goodbye," Penny said. "When did being nice go out of style?" This was why she hadn't had sex in almost a year. It wasn't for lack of trying. She met a lot of guys, but one way or another, they were all jerks.

Where were the nice guys?

"You're too picky," Mya said. "And I mean that in the nicest way. I don't have any issues finding guys to sleep with me."

"Sex with a guy is not the same as finding a nice guy to have dinner with." They'd had this conversion one too many times. She wanted conversation and stimulation of her brain, not just sex.

Mya shrugged. "Your loss. But tell me, does dinner make you scream in pleasure?"

"If it does, remind me not to eat there," Annabelle said, making everyone laugh.

"I don't know," Jodi said. "Sounds like it could be a good

time. If dinner makes you scream in pleasure, imagine what dessert can do."

Everyone laughed, including Penny. Maybe her friends were right. Maybe she needed to stop trying to find stimulating conversation and go for hot sex.

At least then, one part of her would be stimulated.

Chapter Two

Alec

The waves were the one place he felt totally free from stress.

Nothing else mattered when he was out in the water, paddling as fast as he could to catch a wave, struggling to stand.

There was no thought of meetings or reports or data.

It was just him and the waves against the world.

That same feeling he got when he surfed, one of freedom, of lack of control, of pure joy, had just happened to him on dry land.

While staring at a woman.

He'd been mesmerized—that was the only word for it—the second he saw her. She was in the pool, walking along, laughing and chatting. He didn't hear anything she said and had no clue what her voice sounded like, but she'd grabbed his attention in seconds, and he'd been unable to do anything but stare at her.

What the fuck was happening to him?

"I think I'm going to go find that dick, Matt, and see what the fuck he said to those women," his friend and co-worker Ben said. "That gorgeous lady looked ready to murder him."

Finally paying attention, Alec looked at Ben. "Huh?"

"Matt. The asshole who was talking to the girls in the pool. The guy who keeps fucking up reports and drives us crazy at work." Ben shook his head. "Were you paying any attention at all, or were you too busy staring at the brunette in the pool?"

He had him there. "Yeah, I sort of lost focus there for a minute." Something that never happened.

As the director of a team of developers, it was his job to stay on task and be focused. Somehow, one sexy-as-hell woman blew that all up.

"What exactly did Matt do?" he asked Ben.

"I have no clue, but from the looks of it, he opened his mouth and said something stupid, as usual."

It was pretty well known at work that Matt was sexist and was always saying things that would get him in trouble. Alec had written him up twice and wasn't sure why HR hadn't done anything about it. When they got back to the office, he would have to check in and see what the hold-up was.

The company they worked for, Holston Management, had sent the entire IT department on this retreat as a way to thank them for their hard work and accomplishments over the last year. Alec had doubts about letting a hundred tech guys loose on a beach but was relieved when the company planned events for the group. Until they announced that the last two days were open and that employees were free to do whatever they wanted.

The director in him had cringed, and instead of having fun like he should have been doing, he was watching over everyone, ensuring they didn't get into trouble. His own boss, Gabe, had told him to stop worrying and just have fun, but it wasn't in him to do that.

Until now. After seeing the brunette in the water, he didn't give a flying fuck what any of these guys did. His only concern was finding a way to meet her.

He'd never wanted to meet someone so badly in his life. That included the time when he was thirteen, and he met Kobe Bryant.

This felt oddly bigger than that moment.

"We should go back and talk to them," he said, turning his head and glancing back at the pool.

"No, we should not," Ben said sternly.

Although his words might say no, Ben also stared in the direction of the pool for way too long. "Why is that?"

"Because." That was the only word he said.

"Way to use your words, buddy." Behind his sunglasses, Alec rolled his eyes.

"I don't need a reason, I just don't want to. That's all that matters."

Alec would give him that. They'd been friends for a long time, almost ten years. They started at Holsten Management months apart and on different teams. They'd become fast friends and eventually ended up on the same development team. Alec moved through the ranks quickly, eventually ending up as a director, but Ben had preferred to stay in development, where he actually did the work. He was technically Ben's boss, but Alec never had to worry about Ben. He was good at his job and rarely a pain in the ass.

"I need a drink." Since he still had his surfboard, he

added, "Let me go stash my board in my room, and I'll meet you at the lobby bar."

"I think that's where JT and Gabe are," Ben said.

"Even better."

Alec took off toward his room, trying hard not to think about the sexy brunette who made him feel things without ever even having a conversation. At thirty-two, he'd had his fair share of relationships, but he'd never, not even once, looked at a woman and felt such a visceral reaction. In fact, it was the opposite. He needed to talk to a woman several times before even agreeing to a date. It was the same with sex. He'd had a few one-night stands in his life, but most of the time, he liked to know someone before he slept with them.

The way he was infatuated with one look, he had a feeling he'd throw all his usual rules out the window if he ever got a chance with this mystery woman.

It was better if he never saw her again. Nothing would come of one night together. The chances that they lived anywhere close to one another were slim. Hell, she could be from another country while he was just a midwestern guy who liked to surf.

It was settled. He wouldn't search her out, and even if he saw her again, he'd stay far, far away.

Safer for his heart. He'd made it this many years without having it broken; he didn't need to change that.

After storing his surfboard in his room, he grabbed a plain white t-shirt and headed for the lobby bar. He found Ben, along with JT and Gabe, at a small table with drinks already in hand.

"How were the waves this morning?" JT asked as he sat down.

"Decent." JT also liked surfing, but had skipped this morning, choosing a yoga class in the fitness room instead.

"I can't believe you came to a tropical paradise, and you still went and did yoga," Gabe said to JT.

"It burns off the calories I plan to consume today with a large amount of alcohol." JT raised his glass in salute before taking a drink.

JT was also a developer but on another team within the department. He'd worked alongside Gabe before Gabe had made his way up to junior vice president. The four of them were what upper management liked to call 'the future of the company'. None of them cared for the title, but they did like the trust it brought them when working on projects.

"What's the game plan tonight, gentlemen?" Ben asked.

Like himself, Ben worked better with a plan. "What about the steak restaurant for dinner?" Alec suggested.

"I'm always down for steak," Gabe said. "As your boss, don't tell anyone I said this, but thank fuck we have a couple of nights to ourselves."

"You're not my boss," JT said. "But I'll still keep your secret. Mainly because I'm also happy AF that we don't have to do one more team-building exercise with a bunch of people who wouldn't know what team-building meant if it hit them upside the damn head."

"So, steak for dinner, and then we hit the club?" The resort had a nightclub that opened at eleven. Thanks to eight o'clock start times, they'd skipped it their first few nights there. Now that work was finished, Alec wanted to at least check it out.

Not because he really hoped the woman from the pool would be there.

That didn't factor in at all.

"I overheard a couple of guys from my group talking at the last meeting today that they went last night," JT said, shaking his head. "While I won't repeat what they said, it seems that we will have a good time."

"You're like the biggest prude." Gabe shook his head. "Just say there are hot women there. It's not that difficult."

"You know my sister would have my ass if I disrespected women," JT said.

"I forget, why is calling them hot disrespecting them?" Ben asked. "Because from where I stand, I think it's a compliment."

"Agreed," Alec added his two cents. "If a group of women called me hot, I'd take it that way." He wondered if the woman from the pool would think he was hot. It looked like she was staring at him as he stared at her, but with her sunglasses on, he couldn't be sure.

What would happen if he saw her again tonight? Would they talk? Dance? Spend the night together?

Fuck. He had to stop thinking of her. Why was she special? Why had his mind and his dick chosen this one woman out of all the others to obsess over? In two days, he'd be back home in Dublin, Ohio, and she'd be wherever she lived. He'd never see her again.

Hmm. If he was never going to see her again, what was the harm in having just one night with her? It wasn't what he'd prefer, but if that was all he got, or could have, why not take it?

"It's settled then," Gabe said. "Steakhouse for dinner and then the possibility of dancing with hot women at the club after."

Alec nodded in agreement, visions of the only hot

woman he wanted to dance with taking up all the space in his head.

He couldn't wait to find out what color her eyes were. Would they be dark like the night or a gorgeous deep blue like the ocean? What if they were emerald green like the lush grass after a spring rain?

And when the fuck had he started thinking like a poet? If there was ever a sign that he needed to get laid, this was it. He'd been so laser-focused on work and a big project he'd been working on, that all his free time was spent on that.

He tried to think back to the last time he'd had sex. It was with Bethany and they'd dated—or done something loosely like that—for about two months. But that had been before Christmas. It was May.

That was six months ago.

Six months wasn't that long in the grand scheme of things, especially when it was pretty normal for him to go that long or longer without sex. But after seeing that woman in the pool, his dick was making it known that he wanted out to play.

And only she would do.

Chapter Three

Alec

He'd never spent so much time getting ready in his life.

Well, that wasn't entirely true. When he was sixteen and crushing on Olivia Demling, he'd spent hours trying to find the perfect outfit to impress her with.

This felt eerily similar.

He hoped this time it worked out better than it had with Olivia. When he'd walked into the high school gymnasium for the basketball game, head held high and feeling good about the way he looked, he'd been crushed to find Olivia sitting next to Trent Atwood, holding hands.

Since then, he'd stopped worrying and let people, especially women, like him for who he was and not how he was dressed.

Until tonight.

He was only in Cancun for two more days. That meant

he had limited time to gain her attention. Which in turn meant he needed to make an excellent first impression.

Technically, she'd already seen him, or at least he thought she did. Those damn sunglasses she'd had on made it difficult to know for sure.

Choosing another shirt from his suitcase, he pulled it on, looking at himself in the full-length mirror. He wore black dress shorts, a plain teal t-shirt, and a pair of summer slip-on shoes. On a sigh, he ran his hands through his hair, trying to see what she would see when she looked at him.

Did he look casual and relaxed or uptight? This was Mexico. Should he go with sandals for dinner? He had a pair with him but hadn't worn them yet. He had a thing about his feet, and unless he was surfing or getting in the water, he liked them covered.

But would she?

Turning away from the mirror, he picked up another shirt just as a knock sounded on his door. He yanked it open, giving up on his outfit.

He was hoping like hell that he wouldn't be wearing it for too long.

Ben and JT were standing in the doorway? "You ready?" Ben said. "Gabe went ahead so we could get on the list."

Refusing to look in the mirror one last time, Alec grabbed his phone, shoving it into his pocket. "Ready as I'll ever be." The truth in those words were known only to him.

When they reached the steakhouse, Gabe was already seated with a drink in hand.

"No wait?" JT asked.

"None," Gabe answered. "Although I had to tip for them to seat me without you assholes. What took you so long?"

"You have seen this resort, right?" Alec said. "And my room is in the block that's farthest away."

"That's going to wreak havoc tonight when you try and take a girl back to your room," Ben said with a knowing eyebrow raise.

He'd been there when Alec had seen her, and he knew he wanted to see her again just from the way he'd acted. But there was no way he could know just how obsessed he was after only seeing her for a few minutes.

"Maybe she'll take him back to her room," JT suggested. "That's my plan. Then I can leave when it's over."

"Does it make us dicks that we are discussing sleeping with women we've never even met?" Alec asked. Deep down, there was a part of him that thought he should just go back to his room after dinner and skip the club.

"Probably a little," Ben said. "But none of us would do anything if the woman didn't agree. We aren't Matt."

"Wait," Gabe said. "What did Matt do?"

"There were two women in the pool earlier when Alec and I were coming back from the beach and we saw them talking to Matt and Joe. From the looks of it, Matt said something that made one of them angry, and if Joe hadn't pulled him away, that woman might have ripped his head off."

"Fuck," Gabe swore. "I'm sure it was a sexist comment. He's made a few too many of those this year, and nothing's been done even though there have been complaints. It might be time for me to talk to HR and see what can be done." He finished his drink in one gulp. "That fucking asshole is going to ruin my night of fun. I can sense it now."

"There's nothing you can do while we're here," JT said. "Let it go and deal with it when we get back to work."

"I agree with JT," Alec said. "But, if I see him tonight and he makes any sort of sexist comment, I might not be held accountable for my actions."

JT lifted a fist for him to bump, which he did. "Same."

"As your boss, I'm going to advise against that," Gabe said. "But as a person who hates Matt as much as the rest of you," he smirked, "just do it where I won't see it."

"That's permission if I've ever heard it," Ben said, fist-bumping JT and then Alec.

"No, no," Gabe said, "it just gives me plausible deniability," chuckling as he said it.

A few minutes later, after they'd ordered and gotten drinks, Ben was telling a funny story from college when Alec caught a glimpse of bright orange in his peripheral vision. Something inside forced him to glance over, and he was glad he did.

It was the brunette from the pool looking even better than she had in a bikini, in a bright orange, strapless sundress, her brown hair dusting her bare shoulders. Three other women surrounded her, but Alec only saw her.

She and her friends were being shown to a table, which just so happened to be directly next to where he was sitting.

As she sat down, the brunette's gaze landed on his.

Green. Her eyes were green.

She looked unsure at first, but then her mouth tipped into a smile, and she gave a small head nod in his direction. Then she was gone, turning back around to talk to her friends.

His cock was rock hard in his shorts after just one look, one smile, and one head nod.

This one gorgeous woman was going to be his downfall.

And he was sort of looking forward to it.

"Um, excuse me," JT whispered, leaning forward over the table and looking directly at him. "What the hell was that?"

"What was what?" Alec asked, like he hadn't just been eyefucking the brunette.

"Do you know her?" JT asked, eyes wide and full of mischief.

"She's one of the women from the pool today," Ben answered before he could.

JT sat back, looking smug. "Oh, this is interesting. Alec Blair, you're keeping secrets from us."

All four women at the table looked over at JT's raised voice. "There are no secrets, and keep it down," he whisper-shouted.

Gabe, who was seated next to Alex, punched him in the shoulder and then whispered, "Go talk to her."

"She's with her friends. I am not talking to her." Shit, even as the words came out of his mouth, he realized his mistake.

Gabe and JT laughed. On his other side, Ben was oddly silent. It was then that Alec noticed him looking over at the table of women, with one particular woman staring back at him. The other one from the pool. "Maybe you should be harassing him." Alec nodded his head toward Ben.

"Nope, he's obviously interested in the cute redhead," JT said. "You are being cagey."

"Call her cute again," Ben said with a growl, "and I'll punch you in the face."

"Whoa," JT held his hands up in a surrender motion. "There's no need to get violent."

"This gets more interesting by the second," Gabe said. "Did you guys talk to these women?"

Alex shook his head. "No. They were in the pool talking to Joe and Matt."

"And yet," he lowered his voice even more, "the pair of you seem to have some sort of," he paused as if searching for the word, "connection with them."

He gave in, figuring maybe they could help him decipher these strange feelings stirring inside him. "I can't stop thinking about her. It took me twice as long to get ready for dinner because I wanted to impress her if I saw her."

It felt oddly good to say the words out loud. To put it out into the world.

"If that smile she gave you when she sat down is any indication, I'd say it worked," Gabe said.

"That's it?" Alec asked. "You're not going to give me shit, or I don't know, tell me what to do?"

"First of all, why would we give you shit?" JT asked. "We've all lusted after women before. And second, what sort of advice are you looking for here? You're in Cancun. Your only option is to sleep with her and enjoy your one or maybe two nights together before you both go your separate ways."

"If we were home, that advice might be different," Gabe said. "But who knows where she lives, and the odds that it's anywhere near you are not good."

He hated that they both made good points. They were things he'd said to himself, which was why he'd permitted himself to even think of pursuing her. He'd have one or two great nights and then go back to his life in Ohio.

Except, when he saw her walk into the restaurant, his heart beat faster, his palms got sweaty, and his body grew restless. Those were the same things he'd felt when he'd been sixteen and lusting after Olivia Demling.

It had taken months to get over that heartbreak, and he'd never done anything but say a few words to her in Spanish class.

If he somehow convinced this gorgeous woman to sleep with him, he was not equipped to deal with the heartbreak it would cause. Probably why, in the sixteen years since that moment, he'd stayed as far away from anyone who made him feel anything similar.

"What about me?" Ben asked, breaking Alec from his thoughts of the past.

"What about you?" Gabe asked.

"This feels," he looked back over to the table of women," different. How am I supposed to just go about my life after seeing her?"

His words made Alec feel better about his own infatuation with the brunette. Maybe the feelings he was having weren't normal after only seeing someone, but if Ben was having the same type of feelings, maybe they weren't as unusual as he thought.

"Are you guys sitting here telling us that you, what? Fell in love at first sight?" JT asked in obvious disbelief.

"I wouldn't call it love," Ben said, "but it feels so unlike anything I've ever felt that I know it feels wrong to just sleep with her and never see her again."

"I think you both need to take a beat," Gabe said. "Let's finish dinner and hit the club. Hopefully they are there and then you can talk to them and see if the feelings are still there."

Gabe, the wisest of them all, had a point.

Alec just wasn't sure how he was supposed to get

through dinner, with her only feet away from him, her bare shoulders enticing him to put his mouth against her skin and taste her.

Nor was he sure how he was going to be able to eat with a hard-on.

Chapter Four

Penny

She could feel his eyes on her back, and something about it was heady. It was the same feeling she'd gotten when he was watching her in the pool.

And she liked it.

A lot.

Mya leaned forward, her voice a whisper, "That group of guys behind us is hot."

Annabelle was already openly staring at the table, or at least one guy—the guy from the pool who'd been staring at her. Jodi, whose back was also to them, just like her own, turned to glance at them. Penny didn't make a move because she already knew what they looked like—or at least what the one who was staring a hole through her back looked like.

"Is that guy staring at you, Annabelle?" Jodi asked.

"He most definitely is," Mya said. "Do you know him?"

Annabelle shook her head but kept her eyes on the table of guys. "We saw them at the pool today."

"Uh yeah, I don't think so," Mya said. "I was at the pool, and I'd have noticed four sexy as fuck guys if they'd been there."

"It was only two of them, and we saw them while we were in the pool. When Annabelle almost murdered someone," she added, so they knew what she was talking about. "They weren't in the pool, but out of the water towards the edge by the grass."

"From the looks of it," Jodi said, "you made an impression."

Annabelle finally took her eyes off her guy and looked around the table. "That guy, the one with the deep blue eyes, is seriously my fantasy guy. At least in the looks department."

"The key phrase there is looks department," Mya said. "He could be a total asshole in person. And I'm thinking he might be, the way he keeps staring at you."

"I like it," Annabelle said, once again turning her head to look over at the table of guys.

"Who was the other guy at the pool today?" Jodi asked.

"Teal shirt," Annabelle said before Penny could answer.

"And do you like him looking at you?" Jodi asked. "Because if you don't, you're shit out of luck. His eyes are glued to your back."

"He's pretty hot," Penny said, unsure what else to say.

"Good enough for one night of sweaty sex kinda hot, or you'll rub one out while thinking about him hot?" Mya asked.

"Jesus," Penny swore. "Why are we friends again?"

"Because you and your prudish ways would be lost without me," Mya said happily as she popped an olive from her martini into her mouth.

Penny couldn't help but laugh. She wasn't offended by Mya calling her a prude. It was a running joke, but just that, a joke. Her friends knew her well enough to know that wasn't the case. She was just more selective about who she slept with.

When it came to solo fun, she was the queen of vibrators. Really, she was. She had at least a dozen, in all shapes and sizes.

If she wanted an orgasm, she had plenty of ways to get that done.

It was just that sometimes, like now, she'd really like to have a partner to help with that.

"I say go for it," Jodi said. "You deserve some fun after the last few weeks."

Jodi wasn't wrong. The company she worked for had purchased another company and they were laying off employees left and right. Every day, she worried that she'd be on the chopping block to lose her job. So far, she was safe, but it wasn't a foregone conclusion that it would stay that way.

Penny looked at Annabelle. "What do you say? I will if you will."

Annabelle looked back over at the table of guys, biting down on her bottom lip. Penny was silent while she thought about it. "I'm in," she finally said.

"Yay!" Mya cheered as if they'd just won the Olympics.

Penny could only imagine that all the guys were looking in their direction, considering that half the restaurant was doing the same.

"So how do we do this?" Annabelle asked.

Penny thought for a second and then said, "No clue."

"It's like I have to do everything," Jodi said. "We go dancing."

"Oh, yeah," Mya said. "Dancing is seductive and should definitely lead to sex."

"Unless you're me and can't dance," Penny said, waving her hand. She liked to dance but was horrible at it.

Mya cringed. "You're right. I've seen you dance one too many times, and you even make Jodi look good."

"Excuse me," Jodi said, completely offended. "Even I can grind on a guy and get him to come home with me. I've had no complaints."

"Come on," Annabelle said. "You can do this, Pen. You don't have to dance like it's a wedding. You just have to swivel your hips and make him want you."

"It's like sex. I'm going to assume you are pretty good at that, while I have no firsthand knowledge" Jodi said.

Penny groaned. "I mean, I've had no complaints in that department, but it's not as if I'm asking guys to rate my sex skills." Maybe she was overthinking this. Maybe she didn't need to dance with this guy. They could just talk.

She was good at talking.

Her personality was what people—more specifically, guys—liked.

"New plan," she said, lowering her voice so the table of guys, including the one she planned to seduce, couldn't hear. "We will go to the club, and instead of dancing, I will charm him with my words."

Mya cracked a smile, trying hard not to laugh. "Probably a better idea."

Everyone laughed, and for just a little bit, Penny felt confident.

That confidence dissipated when they arrived at the club after dinner.

There were women everywhere. Dressed in a lot less than she was wearing. Why would a guy, specifically the guy she wanted, choose her, when he could choose anyone else?

Looking around, she didn't see him anywhere. He and the rest of the guys at his table had left the restaurant before she and her friends had, but not by much. They'd watched them walk up the stairs toward the club and considering there was nothing else up here, they had to be there somewhere.

"Over there!" Annabelle shouted above the music. It was only nine-thirty but the bass was already pumping with bodies colliding everywhere on the dance floor.

Penny looked to where Annabelle pointed across the room and sure enough, there were the four guys, hers included, standing at the bar. Her thighs clenched at just how sexy he looked. The teal t-shirt he was wearing fit him like a glove, and the color made his skin glow.

She wasn't shy, nor was she insecure about her looks. But hitting on a guy that hot made her nervous. The only thing that had her moving in his direction along with her friends was that this was Cancun. If he rejected her, she'd never have to see him again.

Before they even reached the guys, the one who'd been staring at Annabelle stepped forward. "Hey," he said, his eyes glued to Annabelle. "I'm Ben."

"Annabelle!" she shouted.

Penny watched as the two shook hands and then never let the other go.

A throat cleared near her ear and she glanced up to see her guy only inches from her.

"I'm Alec," he said, his voice loud enough to be heard over the music, but because he was so close, it was almost like a whisper in her ear.

She swallowed, giving herself another second to gain composure. "Penny," she finally said.

He smiled and the gleam in his blue eyes had her asking, "What was that for?"

"What was what for?" he asked, leaning in again to be heard.

"That look when I said my name?" He was so close and the urge to touch him was so strong, but somehow, she held back.

He shrugged. "Your name...it suits you."

"And how exactly would you know that? You just met me." Okay, the nerves were gone, and now she was in her zone.

"You make a good point, but I have a feeling that, like a penny, you're strong, resilient, and good luck." That last word was whispered so close to her ear that she could feel his breath against her skin.

Gathering her courage, she stood up on her tiptoes and leaned into him, so that her mouth was against his ear. "Pennies are only good luck if they are heads up, and sometimes," she paused for dramatic effect, "I like to be facedown."

Being bold was a trait that people either liked or hated. She hoped Alec liked it.

The catch of his breath told her she had him right where she wanted him. From the corner of her eye, she saw his hand reach out as if he was going to touch her, but stopped just before reaching her hip.

His restraint was remarkable if he was feeling anything like she was. Reaching out, she grabbed his hand, placing it on her hip, her eyes holding steady with his, giving him the permission he needed with just a look.

His fingers tightened on her hip. "Dance with me." It wasn't a question, but a command.

The thong she was wearing to avoid panty lines was drenched. She shook her head. "I suck at it." Putting her flaws on display was not the way to get what she wanted.

Which was under him, with his dick deep inside her.

The hand he had on her hip, slipped to her back, just above her ass. The move had him moving even closer to her until their bodies touched. "It's a good thing then that I plan to have you plastered against me so that when I move, you move."

This close, she could see that his eyes were blue. More teal actually. Remarkably similar to the color of his shirt. No wonder it looked good on him. Needing to steady herself, she lifted her arm, placing her hand on his chest. She could feel the beat of his heart pumping fast and it had her wondering if he was as nervous and excited as she was.

When she'd walked into the restaurant and spotted him, the way he'd stared at her made her sure that he'd recognized her from the pool. It felt good to be wanted and at the same time odd that they wanted the same thing.

At least, she hoped they wanted the same thing.

Please God, let him want the same thing.

Chapter Five

Alec

Penny. Her name was Penny, and she was touching him and letting him touch her.

It was everything he wanted and yet, not nearly enough.

"Penny," he said, her name coming out needy and desperate. "Please, dance with me." He hated dancing. Hated being on display where everyone could see him. For Penny, with Penny, he wanted to do it.

He wanted to show everyone that he was the guy she'd chosen and he was the one who'd be balls deep inside her before the night was over.

She nodded, her eyes conveying everything she needed to say without ever speaking a word.

I'll do this for you, with you, because I know you won't let me look out of place.

He'd just met her, and yet he knew from just a look what she was thinking.

With his eyes never leaving hers, he took her hand in his and led her to the floor. The song was fast, but that didn't stop him from taking her in his arms and pressing their bodies together. She wound her arms around his neck, as he settled her body against his. With the sexy heels on her feet, they were only a couple of inches apart in height.

A perfect fit.

His arms were around her waist, his hands unable to keep still on her ass and hips. She was so fucking sexy that he was in a trance as they moved together, grinding and gyrating to the music.

Her confession that she wasn't a good dancer was far from the truth.

She was amazing...at least in his arms.

People bumped into them, and there were voices all around them, but the only thing he cared about was Penny. With her in his arms, he felt free from everything. It felt the same as when he was out on the water with his board. Both in control and out of control at the same time.

There was no way she couldn't feel his cock, hard and pressed up against her body. It took all his control to stop his hands from moving lower, to touch the bare skin of her thighs that were exposed thanks to her very short dress.

Suddenly, he needed to know more about her than her name and how she felt pressed up against his body.

Leaning in, he let his lips trail over her ear before asking, "Wanna get out of here?"

She pulled back, her eyes glassy with need, but also with uncertainty.

Shit, he'd fucked up. "To talk," he said loud enough so she could hear. "Maybe just out on the balcony?"

She looked over to the glass doors that led to the balcony

before looking back at him and nodding. Taking her hand in his, he pulled her from the dance floor, across the room and outside, where fresh ocean air and only remnants of the loud bass greeted them.

"Wow," she said, her voice still a little loud since they'd had to practically yell to be heard. She laughed. "Sorry," she said, her voice a few decibels lower," I didn't realize just how loud it was in there."

"Me neither." He hadn't let go of her hand and was running his thumb back and forth over her knuckles, unwilling to stop touching her. "Wanna sit or..." He trailed off, not even sure what he was going to say.

"I'm good standing. But let's go over here." This time, it was her pulling him as they moved to the railing where they could look out over the whole resort. "This view is amazing."

"You're telling me." He wasn't looking at the resort or the ocean. He was looking at her. It was ridiculous how much she turned him on. How much he wanted her. He'd dated pretty women before, but Penny wasn't merely pretty. He didn't know anything about her and yet, he knew, down to his core, that she was smart and funny and vivacious and interesting.

How he knew was an enigma to him.

"So," she said, turning to face him again. "What brings you to Cancun?"

"I was here for work. My company had a retreat, but they gave us the last two days off to enjoy the trip."

"Wait," she narrowed her eyes, "are you talking about the tech retreat?"

"That's the one. How do you know about that?" She was so cute the way she shook her head and rolled her eyes.

"My friends and I had heard that was why the pool was so busy today. I can't believe you're in tech."

He raised a questioning eyebrow. "Why is that?" He couldn't wait to hear her answer.

"You've seen you, right?" She raked her eyes up and down his tall frame, from his feet to his head. "You don't really fit the mold." Her perusal of him, had him standing a little taller.

He laughed. "Because I've obviously seen sunlight before and I don't dress like it's the eighties, I can't be in tech?"

"You said it." Her smirk was sexy as fuck and all he could think about was wiping it off with his mouth.

He pulled her just a little closer until her face was right in front of his, only inches away. "What if I told you I play an enormous amount of video games and love sci-fi movies."

Her free hand, the one he wasn't holding, grazed up his arm, stopping before reaching his shoulder. "I'd say you're just like every other guy I know."

He dipped his face even closer until his lips barely brushed hers. He heard her intake of breath, and his cock got even harder at the sound. "Do any of those guys make your panties wet?" He didn't know if her panties were wet, but he had to assume they were if she was feeling anything like he was.

Another smirk. "You presume a lot. Maybe I'm not even wearing anything under this dress." Her lips pressed just a little more against his. "Then again, maybe I am."

They were both breathing heavily, and he wasn't even sure how he was still standing since all the blood in his body was now in his dick. He let his hand trail down her back and over her ass until it came to the edge of her dress. His senses kicked in just enough to know that they were very exposed and anyone would be able to see him fondling her ass where they were standing.

He didn't want that.

He walked her backward, their lips still touching although not really kissing, until her back hit the wall. It gave them a little more privacy. Once there, his hand continued his journey. He found her bare leg, reveling in the feel of it against his palm, before moving it higher under her dress.

When he came into contact with bare ass, he lost it. He crushed his mouth against hers, no longer able to hold himself back.

She didn't seem to care.

The kiss was desperate and furious, each of them tugging the other closer until there was no space left between their bodies. Her lips were soft and silky and held just a small taste of tequila.

He couldn't get enough.

"Alec," she moaned when he kneaded her ass in his palm as he trailed his mouth to her neck.

"I should spank your ass for walking around with no panties on," he murmured against the sensitive skin of her neck. He'd never been so bold as to say something like that to a woman he just met. Penny was different.

"Ch-check again," she said, breathlessly.

Her meaning sank in.

God in heaven and everything that was holy, she was wearing a thong. His hand moved up a little higher on her ass, and sure enough, there was the band at her hips. Giving it a small tug, she moaned loudly. That small tug of the fabric had its desired effect, rubbing against her pussy.

So he did it again, with a little more force and before she

could moan into the night where anyone walking by below could hear, he took her mouth in another kiss.

Her hips jerked against his cock, desperately searching for relief. He knew the feeling. His dick had never been harder, and all he wanted in the world was to strip her naked and fuck her madly.

But not there.

He needed privacy for what he wanted to do to her.

"Come back to my room with me," he murmured against her lips. "Please," he added, desperate for her to say yes.

"Yes," she said, her voice sounding just as desperate.

Having the answer he wanted, he wasted no time getting them back inside so they could get out of the club and get to his room as fast as possible. Only the universe had other plans.

"Blair!" he heard his last name being called, and like the dumbass he was, he looked over and saw JT coming toward him.

"Fuck!" he swore. Turning to Penny, he said, "Looks like we aren't going to get to escape."

She laughed but leaned in, her mouth to his ear. "A small delay will only add to the anticipation."

He groaned as his cock pulsed with need in his shorts.

JT reached them, placing a hand on Alec's shoulder. "Aren't you going to introduce me?" His voice was charming as usual, even if it was loud to be heard over the pulsing beat of the music.

Fucking cockblocker was what he was.

"This is Penny," he said. "Penny, this is my friend, JT."

"Nice to meet you!" she shouted happily.

"You too," JT said. "I met your friend Mya a little bit ago."

"Do you know where she went?" Penny asked.

JT turned to look out over the dance floor, Penny and Alec following the direction of his gaze. Turns out there was no need to look for her because she and one of the other women who had been sitting with Penny at dinner were walking in their direction.

His night of sex with Penny was looking less and less like it was going to happen.

"Hey!" Penny said when her friends reached them.

"And just where have you been, little missy," one of the women said.

Penny laughed, shaking her head. "Guys, this is Alec." She placed her free hand on his chest. "These are my friends Mya and Jodi." She pointed to each woman as she said their name.

Alec shook both of their hands. "Nice to meet you." Just as he said the words, Gabe joined them.

"Looks like a party, and yet, no one invited me," he said with a wink.

"This is Gabe," Alec told Penny, who shook Gabe's hand.

"Should we get out of here so it's easier to talk?" JT asked.

"One of the bartenders told me about a secret spot that rarely anyone goes to," the blonde named Jodi said.

"Of course, you know about a secret spot," the other woman, Mya, said.

Alec looked at Penny, who was wearing an expression that matched his own. Resigned, they agreed and the group left the club together. Alec slowed Penny so they fell a little behind the rest of the group.

"Would it be rude if we just slipped away?"

She stopped walking, turning to face him. "Yes, but my friends would understand."

Alec sighed, dropping his forehead to hers. "I want you." Those words were as honest as he'd ever been with someone he'd just met.

"When do you leave?" she asked.

"Day after tomorrow."

"So tonight, we hang with our friends, and pick this up tomorrow." She paused. "If we both still want to."

He closed the distance between their mouths, kissing her deeply but quickly. "Oh, I want to."

"I'm just saying if you change your mind..." Her words trailed off.

"I'm not changing my fucking mind. I've been hard since I saw you in the pool today." To show her just what he was talking about, he pressed himself into her body, his erection easily noticeable. "This is happening."

"Are you two coming?" a woman's voice shouted.

"Not yet," he said against Penny's lips. "But soon."

Taking her hand back in his, they started walking again. As much as he wanted her, he liked the idea of getting to know her just as much.

Well, not just as much, but it was pretty close.

Chapter Six

Penny

Over the years, there had been very few times where her friends hadn't been able to read the room.

This was one of those times.

Couldn't they see how badly she and Alec wanted to be alone? Were they oblivious to sexual tension? It sure as hell seemed like it.

There would come a time where each of them would need her to do the same and she damn well was going to cockblock them just like they were doing to her.

Except for Annabelle. Apparently she and the Ben guy were off doing who knows what somewhere.

Penny knew what. It was the same what that she wanted to be doing.

"Tell me about your friend that's with my friend," Penny asked as they walked in a big group toward wherever this secret spot Jodi was leading them to was.

"Ben," Alec said. "He's a good guy."

"The best," one of the other guys said from in front of them. She believed it was the one named JT but couldn't be totally sure.

"Stop worrying about Annabelle," Jodi said. "I can track her if we need to."

"You can track your friend?" the other guy, Gabe, asked.

"We all can," Mya said. "It's just good sense."

"I'm sort of offended that none of you fools track me," JT turned around walking backward so he could see everyone. "I could have been abducted and no one would be the wiser."

"I wish someone would abduct you," Alec said.

"Ahh, is someone sad he's not still on the balcony making out?" JT rubbed his eyes like a crying baby and Penny couldn't stop her giggle.

"Whoa!" Gabe said. "Blair was making out? Is the world ending?" He ducked and covered his head. "Are meteors falling from the sky?"

"I fucking hate both of you," Alec said, making Penny giggle again.

"I too saw the making out," Mya said.

"Great," Alec whispered under his breath.

"It's cool," Penny told him, squeezing his hand in hers and leaning into his side more. "It's not as if we were invisible."

He slowed his walk, cupping her cheek in his hand and bringing his lips to hers. "I wish we were." The kiss was gentle and sweet, and nothing like what they'd done on the balcony.

The difference between the two was shocking and yet,

for the life of her, Penny couldn't decide which one she liked more.

"Hello!" she heard Mya shout. "No more kissing!"

"Ignore them," Alec said, his lips still touching hers, if only barely.

She fisted his shirt in her hand, pulling him closer. "Screw waiting until tomorrow. Let's just walk away. What can they do?"

His eyes were dark with need, and just as he was about to kiss her again, and she knew down to the soles of her feet that it would be amazing, a hand landed on his shoulder, pulling him away from her.

"None of that," Gabe said.

Alec groaned, giving Penny a frustrated look.

"This is it!" Jodi shouted as they walked under a stone archway.

The space was small, but it was obviously a bar set back in what could be considered an alcove. There were a few people inside, but that was it.

"I take back everything I was thinking," JT said.

"Wait," Jodi stopped to face him. "What were you thinking?"

"That you had no clue where you were taking us and we'd all end up dead or at the least maimed." Gabe sauntered by her, making Jodi frown at him.

"I always know what I'm doing," she said, obviously annoyed.

"Is he always an ass?" Penny asked Alec.

"Yes," he answered.

"Let's sit there." Mya pointed to a group of comfy looking couches and chairs in the corner.

They followed her over and Alec pulled Penny down

with him so that she was in his lap. "If we can't be alone, this is the next best thing," he whispered in her ear.

She wiggled a little, feeling his dick, which was definitely hard, against her ass. "I see you're still having that same problem you've had since you first saw me."

His arm wrapped around her waist, holding her tightly against him. "I'm starting to think it's less of a problem and more of a reward."

She leaned back against him, laughing. "I think that's supposed to be my line."

The bartender walked over, taking everyone's drink order. Penny went with a tequila and soda since she'd already been drinking tequila. It was a favorite of hers anyway and she knew that she could handle it.

Alec went with a beer.

"Okay," Mya said when the bartender walked away. "What's everyone do for a living?"

Mya was curious by nature, so it wasn't a surprise that she asked a question.

"We work in IT," JT was the first to answer.

"Wait, are you kidding?" Mya reached out an arm, touching JT on the chest.

"I'm not sure why that would be a joke," Gabe said.

"She doesn't mean it like that." Penny could hear the frustration in Jodi's voice. "It's just that we saw a lot of IT guys at the pool today and you three and your friend Ben are not the same as those guys."

"Those guys work with us and most of them are good guys. Minus Matt," Alec said.

"Matt is the one who was an ass to Annabelle," Penny added for clarification.

"That guy was a douche of the highest order," Mya said.

"You won't hear us disagree," JT said. "Gabe is going to find a way to fire him when we get back."

"You have that power?" Jodi asked, looking at Gabe.

"Technically I do, but I have to go through HR."

"He's a VP," Alec said. "He can fire him."

"You're a VP?" Jodi said, her eyes wide, the statement sounding a little condescending.

Penny saw Gabe's back stiffen and instantly knew that Jodi had pissed him off. To try and defuse the situation, she spoke up. "I work in finance."

Mya gave her a look that told her she knew exactly what she was doing. "And I'm also in IT. I'm a developer."

"Me too," JT said, high fiving her.

Alec, obviously catching on, said, "I still develop some, but as a director, I mostly manage people."

"I think that just leaves you, Jodi," JT said.

"Jodi has the coolest job of all," Penny said.

"What do you do?" Alec asked.

"I work in PR for a hockey team." She said it like it wasn't a big deal, but it was.

Not only was she in PR, but at the age of twenty-five, she was the manager of the PR team. It was a big feat at such a young age. "She's being modest," Penny said. "She's the manager of PR and she kicks ass at it."

"Which team?" Gabe asked.

"The Columbus Thunder," Jodi answered.

Alec sat up, Penny shifting on his lap. "Hold up. Columbus as in Ohio?" He wasn't looking at Jodi but at her.

"Yeah, why?"

"And you live there too?" His eyes were wide and full of excitement.

She nodded, unsure what was happening.

"I live in Dublin."

The shock that went through her body was like a blast from a bomb. "There's no way." She turned her body as much as she could in his lap, without actually straddling him so that she was fully looking at him.

Behind her, she vaguely heard someone speak, but she wasn't listening. All she cared about was Alec.

"I can't believe this," he said, his voice just above a whisper, in awe.

"Is this a...bad thing?" She had no clue what he was thinking. This was meant to be a vacation fling, but now that they knew they lived only miles apart, he might not want to see her when they got home.

If it was up to her, she wanted to see him.

He dropped his forehead to hers. "It's the best thing." He took a deep breath like he was going to say something else, but instead he kissed her hard and quick.

She clung to him, not wanting to let go. At least not yet.

She wasn't naive, she knew people lied to get what they wanted. Both men and women. But she didn't think he was lying. He seemed genuine and like he really would want to see her again when they left their tropical paradise.

She was going to choose to believe him.

It was either that or walk away now. Because she knew that once they slept together, it would only be harder to let him go.

Chapter Seven

Alec

There was so much more he wanted to say to Penny. He wanted to tell her that he'd been sick inside at the thought of never seeing her again, that she made him feel different from anything he'd ever felt.

But it was too early.

He had no clue what would come of them being together, or if there was even going to be a them. He just knew that he wanted to try, and now that he knew she lived so close to him, he was going to give it his all.

Because there was no way that these feelings were something that happened all the time. He realized that they had to mean something.

"I really can't believe you live in Dublin," she said. "I go there all the time." She sat up straight on his lap, his dick taking notice at the movement. "Wait, where do you work?"

"Holston Management."

She slapped his chest. "I've been there!"

He laughed, but was also a little annoyed that he never saw her when she'd been there. He could have had her in his life that much sooner. "When?"

"I interviewed there right out of college. Ultimately, I turned it down to work at B&L, but Holston was a close second."

It was his turn to be surprised. "You work at B&L Finance?"

"I do," she said with a big smile. "Why do I have a feeling you're about to say something crazy."

"Because he is," JT plopped down next to them. "He interned there in college."

"Only for a summer," Alec told her. "They were good to me but I wanted to try more than one place to get a feel for what I liked."

Penny stared at him, a look of disbelief in her eyes. This was all so surreal. They'd been practically missing each other for years. Although he was definitely older than her.

"How old are you?" he asked.

"Twenty-five. What about you?"

"Thirty-two." Seven years was a lot, but not too much.

Or was it?

"Is that an issue?" He sensed her hesitance at his age.

She shrugged. "I don't think so. I mean, we're both adults, right?" Those were the words she said, but it seemed like she wasn't sure. He'd never dated anyone that many years younger. A few years, yes, but seven years...that felt like a lot.

"Right," he said. "For the record, I've never dated anyone as young as you, but I'm not against it."

"I feel like I should step in and slow this down," Jodi said. She sat down on the other side of them.

"I agree," Gabe said from nearby. Alec saw him give Jodi a strange look and wondered what that was all about. But only for a second before their words sank in.

"Why?" he asked.

"You guys just met like an hour ago and you're already talking about dating," Jodi said. "That might go down as the fastest courtship in history."

"Probably not," Mya said. "Not if you consider royals and the fact that they married without ever meeting."

"I don't think that counts," JT said.

"Enough," Alec said, firmly, but not in a shout, "Penny and I don't need anyone to step in, and we definitely don't need anyone to slow us down. We are adults and can make our own decisions."

Jodi, obviously not used to being told what to do, lifted an eyebrow and opened her mouth to say something, but before she could, Gabe spoke. "Noted. We will all back off." He turned to look at Jodi, who took a few seconds but reluctantly nodded.

"I gotta say," Mya said. "That was hot." She fanned herself with her hand.

Alec looked at Penny. "Was it?" he asked her.

"Oh yeah," she answered. She leaned in, whispering in his ear for only him to hear. "So hot that I think maybe you should accompany me to find a bathroom."

He groaned, immediately standing, lifting her up, and helping her to her feet. "Penny has to use the restroom."

He didn't wait for anyone to say anything. He just took her hand and pulled her along with him as she laughed uncontrollably.

He heard Jodi say something about the nearest restroom

being behind them, but that wasn't the direction they were going, and neither he nor Penny were listening.

They weren't looking for a restroom. They just wanted a quiet corner where they could be alone for a few minutes.

They turned a corner, and Alec pulled Penny against his body as his back fell against a wall. He had no idea where they were and didn't care. As long as they were alone, that's all that mattered.

His lips were on hers before she could protest or ask what was going on, and the kiss was rough and needy and everything he needed from her. Whenever he kissed her, he felt like she knew exactly what he needed, when he needed it.

This woman, who he'd only technically met just over an hour ago, knew him as well as he knew himself.

If he wasn't horny as fuck, he might stop to consider why and how that was.

"I need to touch you," he murmured as his lips trailed down her jaw.

His hands were on her bare legs, and because she obviously wanted to be touched as much as he wanted to touch her, she lifted a leg and wrapped it around his waist.

That's when the passion took over, and minds shut down.

He spun them quickly, pressing her against the wall and hiking her legs up around his waist. Both his hands were now on her bare ass, his fingers trailing between her legs in search of her already wet and waiting pussy as he pressed his body against hers.

She bucked against him as his mouth kissed every part of available skin on her neck and shoulders. Their combined moans filled the space around them, neither one of them seeming to care.

All he wanted was to make her feel good. Nothing else mattered.

"Alec, please," she begged as her body pressed against his.

"I know what you need, baby." His fingers delved between her legs, and then he was there, right at her entrance, pushing her thong aside and slipping his fingers inside her.

She gasped at the invasion, making him gentle his touch. She was having none of that. She gyrated her hips, pushing his fingers even deeper.

"Shit, you're so wet. So turned on. That's so goddamn hot." He pumped his fingers in and out several times.

She was humping his hand furiously now, searching for her release. The sensations of how much she wanted him were overwhelming, and it all felt too good. His lips on her neck, her legs around his body, and his fingers in her pussy. When his thumb stroked over her clit, once, twice, he knew she was close.

When she came, she pressed her face into his neck, biting his skin, but he didn't care. She could do whatever she wanted to him.

He held her tightly, his fingers still inside her as she slowly came back to reality.

"Jesus, please tell me you don't always go off so quick," he said, dragging his fingers from her body, instantly missing her hot, wet pussy.

She lifted her head from the crook of his neck, taking in his face. "I never have before."

Between them, his dick was still hard and needed attention. She lowered her legs to the ground and then bent like she was going to her knees.

If he was being honest, he badly wanted to see her mouth wrapped around his dick. It was an image that had his dick getting even harder. But this wasn't the time nor place.

"No," he said, grabbing her and hauling her up against him.

She searched his eyes. "It's only fair. I came, so should you."

He groaned. "If you touch my dick out here, I'll have you naked and fucking you against this wall." He pressed his forehead against hers. "I refuse to fuck you against the wall." He kissed her hard. "The first time," he added when he pulled away.

She let out a throaty laugh. "What you're saying is the second or third time is okay to fuck me against the wall?"

He grabbed her hand, pulling her away from the wall. "Fix your dress." She looked down and saw that her dress was still bunched around her waist. She fixed it immediately, with one hand, since he had no plans to give her the other one back. He liked holding her hand in his. Being allowed to touch her in any way made him feel ten feet tall.

"And yes, the second or third or seventy-fifth time, I will fuck you against the wall." He knew instantly that she understood what he was saying because she glanced at him with a look of shock on her face.

It would be at least a couple of months to hit that number unless they were fucking three or four times a day. Something he would be okay with. The comment was made to let her know he was serious about seeing her once they were back home.

He wasn't an expert on other guys or what they did or

didn't do when they were seeing someone. A lot of guys lied to get into women's pants.

Not him. Hopefully, his comment gave her that peace of mind.

When they returned to where their friends were, everyone seemed to be getting along. Everyone except Gabe. He was sitting a few feet away from JT, Mya and Jodi, just watching them.

Or maybe he was only watching Jodi.

Alec couldn't be sure, but Gabe seemed to dislike Jodi, but also wasn't able to look away from her. This was a development that Alec would definitely be asking his friend about when they were alone.

"How was the bathroom break?" Mya asked, waggling her eyebrows.

Penny flipped her friend off while Alec just smiled. They sat back down, this time with Penny next to him. He wrapped his arm around her shoulders, pulling her against his side so they were touching.

"Anyone heard from Ben and Annabelle?" Penny asked.

"I just checked, and at least her phone is in her room," Jodi said.

"From the way Ben was acting," JT said, "I'm guessing she's not alone in that room."

"We don't know that," Gabe said.

Alec was only half paying attention to the conversation thanks to Penny's hand resting on his knee. It was only inches from his dick making it too hard to think of anything else. The regret of not just going back to his room was strong. So strong that he was tempted to throw her over his shoulder and go there now.

They remained in the little alcove bar for another hour before calling it a night.

"Can I walk you to your room?" he asked Penny when they stood up.

She leaned in, her hand on his chest. "I guess it depends. What happens when we get there?"

He wasn't sure what answer she wanted. Did she want sex, or was that moving too fast? He'd already fingered her, and she'd tried to suck his dick. Did that mean sex was back on the table? If the choice was his, he'd stay and make her come a dozen different ways.

The only thing he knew was that he didn't want just one night with her.

"I won't lie and tell you that I don't want to stay with you." He pressed his pelvis against her body. "You can feel how much I want you. That's not in question. But I also don't want to fuck this up." He hoped like hell she'd like his honesty.

She trailed her fingers up over his chest to his neck. "There's a part of me that wants you in my bed tonight." She paused, her expression changing just a little. "But there's also a part of me that is afraid that everything you're saying is just to get into my bed, and then you'll leave, and I'll never see you again."

He hated that she thought that. There was an easy fix, though. "Then it's settled. I'll walk you to your room, kiss you goodnight, and leave." He'd do whatever it took to make her see he wasn't playing around.

What looked a little like relief washed over her face. "I'd like that."

Taking her hand in his, they began to walk toward her room. She was in the opposite direction of his room, but he didn't care. He wanted to spend as many minutes with her as possible.

"Meet me for breakfast in the morning," he said, not really asking and hoping she didn't think he was a dick for his demand.

"Didn't you say you were planning to surf in the morning?"

He'd made the offhand comment during general conversation, but he liked that she remembered. "I can skip it."

She grinned at him. "Or, you could take me with you and let me watch." Her eyes held excitement.

"You want to watch me surf?"

"Yes," she practically moaned, the sound taking his dick from already hard to impossibly hard.

He wasn't sure how he'd be able to look effortless and athletic with her eyes on him as he surfed, but if she wanted to watch, she'd get to watch. "I'll come by and get you on my way to the beach."

"I can just meet you there."

He looked over at her, giving her a stern look. "I will come and get you. After that, we'll go to breakfast."

She nodded, biting down on her lower lip. From the little time he'd spent with her, he knew without a doubt that was a sign she was turned on.

Apparently, she liked when he was demanding and forceful.

That was not going to be a problem.

Chapter Eight

Penny

I t was her last full day of vacation. She should still be snuggled in her comfy bed, fast asleep, dreading going home.

Instead, she was dressed in a bikini with a light summer dress pulled over it, waiting impatiently for Alec to knock on her door so she could watch him surf.

Their night together replayed in her head on repeat. It was a wonder she'd even gotten any sleep for how much she'd thought of him. She couldn't stop remembering the way it felt to be wrapped around his body with his hands on her. Or the way he'd made her come by barely doing anything at all.

She didn't have problems orgasming with a partner, not really. It usually just took a little longer to get there. Not with Alec. It was like he knew her body better than she did.

She wasn't sure why she'd turned down the chance to have him in her bed other than, she somehow wanted to test him. To see what he'd do and say. And, of course, he passed that test with flying colors.

He'd seemed genuine when he'd said he'd wait and that only made her want him more.

She was still in shock that they lived not only in the same state but also only miles apart. She'd been resigned to a one-night stand and now she was going to get to see him again. At least, it seemed that way.

The loud knock on her door startled her, and she looked at the bedside clock to see that it was seven-forty-nine. He was eleven minutes early.

Giddy with excitement, she pulled open the door. She was just about to greet him when he grabbed her by the waist, pulling her against him and kissing her soundly.

This was a greeting she could get behind.

Her arms went around his neck, and she hung on to him as he continued to kiss her. When his kisses slowed, and he finally pulled away, he was smiling.

"I've been thinking about that all night," he said.

Her arms were still around his neck, and because she could, she toyed with his hair. "Do you see me complaining?" She could have told him that she felt the same. That it had been hard to sleep after the goodnight kiss he'd given her at the door.

But she kept that to herself.

She didn't want to seem overzealous or eager.

"Are you ready?"

She nodded, picking up her small crossbody bag next to the door. She didn't think she'd need it, but it held her phone and some sunscreen. "Where's your surfboard?" She made sure the door closed and then took his outstretched hand. The man really did like to hold her hand.

"I dropped it down at the beach before coming to get you. A few guys are already out, and they said they'd watch it for me."

"Did you bring that with you from Ohio, and how do you enjoy surfing when you live in Ohio?" She had so many questions.

He laughed. "Yes, I brought it with me. It's a pain to check at the airport, but I have a case for it. As for why I enjoy surfing." He shrugged. "My mom is from California, and we went back every summer to visit family until I was in college. She taught me, and since then, I have tried to catch waves whenever possible."

"That's pretty cool. This is only the second time in my life I've ever even seen the ocean."

He stopped walking, gawking at her. "What?"

"My family never really took vacations, but if we did, we went somewhere we could drive in a few hours. Tennessee, Michigan...places like that." Somehow admitting that made her feel younger than her twenty-five years.

"That's settled. You aren't going to watch me surf." His eyes sparkled. "You're going to do it."

He started walking again, this time fast, and since he was still holding her hand, she had no choice but to practically jog to keep up with him. "I don't think that's a good idea. I doubt I'd be any good at it."

"Doesn't matter. I have one day to show you what you've been missing out on all these years. Surfing is the best way to do that."

"I don't look at it as missing out. If you don't know what you're missing, you're not really missing anything, right?"

He looked at her again, his mouth open, but this time he kept walking. "Wrong. That's not at all how it works." They reached the beach and what was presumably his surfboard. "It doesn't matter if you're good or bad at surfing. What matters is that you understand how amazing and profound the ocean and waves are."

The way he said it, how he sounded like it was the most important thing, had her agreeing readily. "This is your idea, and when I drive you crazy because I don't listen or can't stand up, it's on you." There went her chances of sleeping with him. No man wanted to have sex with a woman after watching her fall off a surfboard and listening to her bitch about falling.

Why had she agreed to this again?

"You won't drive me crazy, and if you don't ever stand up, it won't matter. It's the experience that counts." He led her over to a cabana that was lined with numerous surf-boards. "Let's get you a board and a wetsuit. While I'm going to appreciate whatever swimsuit you have on under that dress," his eyes roamed up and down the length of her body, "I'm positive it's not suitable for surfing."

Chills ran through her body at his sensual gaze. "How do you know I'm wearing anything under this dress?" If he was going to turn her on, she was going to do the same. Two could play this game.

He growled, literally growled, gripping her around the waist and pulling her against him. "Are you trying to get me to fuck you right here?" The dirty words were whispered in her ear for only her to hear.

She was on fire. That was the only way to explain what she said next. "I'm sort of afraid that once you try to teach me to surf, you'll change your mind and never want to see me again." Apparently, when she was turned on, she became extremely honest.

He pulled back just enough to look at her face. Confusion was written all over his face. "That's not possible."

"You don't know that. I'm sort of defiant when learning something new." That was an understatement. She was reluctant to change and completely uncooperative. It was her worst trait, and she'd tried many times to change but it never took.

"I don't care. Be defiant. I'll still want to fuck you." The statement was made with so much certainty and confidence that she wondered if maybe he'd like it if she was a little defiant.

Hmmm. That was something new. Something unexpected

Something she might also like.

After getting her all geared up with a wetsuit and surfboard, he went over a few general pieces of information. She listened intently but was distracted by how good he looked without a shirt on.

This was going to be harder than she thought.

"Let's try a few pop-ups on dry land so you get the feel of it," he said. Both their boards were flat on the sand, and he instructed her to lie down. "Lay down on your stomach."

She did as he asked, with him moving to stand above her. "Scoot up just a little." She felt his hand on her waist as he helped her move. "You need to be in the sweet spot so that when you pop up to your feet, you're right where you need to be." His words were seductive even if they weren't meant to be, and his hands lingered on her body longer than needed, but she wasn't complaining. "Perfect. Now you're going to pop up to your feet quickly and gain your balance." He moved over to his board, lying down in a position similar to hers.

"You're going to pop up to your feet like this." He moved swiftly, going from his belly to his feet in the blink of an eye. She watched his feet and body, taking in the small details of how he moved.

When she was ready, she mirrored what he did, popping quickly to her feet.

"Good," he praised her. "That's really good. Do it a few more times to make sure you know what it feels like."

The way he praised her made her feel like a queen, and because she wanted to hear the words again, she made sure she did it the same way each time.

"That's really good. You look like a natural." He was smiling as he watched her, and she got the sense that he meant what he was saying.

He didn't strike her as someone who would lie just to make her feel good.

"On land," she remarked. "There's no guarantee I'll be able to do this in the ocean."

"Have more faith," he said. "I've seen people who were great athletes fail on a surfboard and people who seemed clumsy on dry land succeed. It's more about being one with the wave than being athletic."

She cocked her head to the side. "I didn't peg you as someone who is all zen and goes with the flow."

He laughed. "I'm not, usually. But when it comes to surfing, it's the only way to be."

"So the stereotype of the laid-back surfer dude is real?"

"One hundred percent." He pulled his wetsuit all the way on, covering his sexy chest, then bent down, picking up his board. "Grab your board. We're going to hit the water."

She groaned but did as he asked. She had the basics

down, but she just knew that at some point, she was going to go off and yell at him.

It was uncontrollable.

He'd already explained how to get out into the water with a board, but he explained it again as they went without any hint of annoyance as they moved through the water.

She was beginning to realize that he was a good teacher.

She followed his directions as she laid down on her board and then as he showed her how to paddle. He wanted her to try paddling several times before she attempted to stand.

He told her when to go, and she paddled like a mad woman.

"That's too much," he said. "Easy and strong."

"I was going easy and strong." She knew her words were clipped, but again, she couldn't help it.

"No, you were erratic and too fast. Let's do it again."

Fifteen times later and somehow, he was still as calm as ever when she was beyond frustrated.

"I'm never going to get it!" She slammed her hand down on the water.

"Penny," he said her name tenderly as he moved in front of her. "You need to relax."

"How can I relax when I suck at this?"

"You don't suck. I actually think I'm going about this the wrong way."

"How can you say that? You're being so patient, and I'm just a mess."

"I think that maybe you just need to do it. Practicing is just making you worse."

She frowned. "But what if I fall?" She wasn't afraid, not really but it was still scary.

"You will, that's just what happens. Very few people stand up their first time."

"So what you're saying is that I will fail but that since everyone does it doesn't really matter?" While not motivational, it made her feel a lot better.

"Pretty much."

She thought about that for a few seconds. It made an odd sort of sense, and since she was no quitter, she was willing to try. "Okay, I'm in." She jumped back on her board, laying on her stomach.

He leaned toward her, lacing his hands on the front of her board. "You can do this." His faith in her gave her strength.

He jumped on his own board, moving several feet away from her. He'd explained that when surfing, you didn't want to be too close to another surfer so you didn't run into each other.

"Wait for the wave!" he shouted. "Trust yourself."

She gave him one last glance before looking back and seeing a wave she wanted. She started paddling, remembering what he'd told her about her strokes. Her arms were tired, and she desperately wanted to quit, but she wasn't going to.

If Alec believed in her, she could believe in herself.

She heard him shout something but blocked it out as she got herself ready to pop up. Timing was everything from what he'd told her, and she didn't want to miss her moment.

When she saw the wave, she let instinct kick in and popped up to her feet. For a second, she thought, she was going to fall, but then she cleared her mind and relaxed her body.

And before she knew what was happening, she found

herself riding the wave. Joy like she'd never felt rushed through her.

She'd done it.

She'd stood up on a surfboard. The feeling was euphoric and beyond anything else she'd ever felt.

"You did it!" Alec shouted as he raced toward her in the water. "You fucking did it!" Then she was in his arms, clutching him as he spun her around in a circle. When the spinning stopped, his mouth descended on hers, as he kissed her passionately.

She clawed at him, wanting him closer, loving the feel of his strong body against hers.

"You're amazing," he said, pulling back and dropping his forehead against hers as he cupped her cheek in his hand.

Riding high off her accomplishment, she gave in to everything she was feeling. "Alec, I want you." She didn't want to wait anymore. She wanted this man, and she wanted him now.

His eyes flared with heat. "Are you sure?"

That he even had to ask, told her she was doing the right thing. "Don't make me wait any longer."

With the efficiency of a man who was about to get laid, he returned her surfboard and wetsuit, grabbed his own board and bag, and with her hand gripped in his, walked at a brisk pace toward what she assumed was his room.

Neither spoke since they both knew what the plan was.

To get naked as fast as possible.

After that, they'd figure it out.

When they reached his room, he practically threw the door open, shoving his surfboard and bag inside and then pulling her with him. When the door closed, she was pushed up against it with his mouth latched to her neck.

"You're so fucking hot, and I can't believe you stood up on that board your first time." His words turned her on almost as much as his mouth against her skin did.

"It was you," she moaned out as he pulled her dress down so he could reach the swell of her breast. "You are the one who believed in me, and that gave me the confidence to do it."

He lifted his head, his eyes meeting hers, but he didn't speak. For long seconds, he just stared at her. Then he finally spoke. "I believed in you because I know you. And that may sound stupid when we just met yesterday, but it's true. You needed encouragement and instruction. Not me screaming half-directions at you. I'm the same way." He paused, shaking his head, a small smile on his lips. "I see so much of myself in you."

His words had her heart beating faster in her chest. She wasn't sure what to say, which was a first, and because of that, she decided actions were better than words.

In one swift motion, she had her sundress off, standing before him in only her bikini. A bikini that showed her curves. She wasn't extremely well endowed in the chest area. A nice B cup, possibly C on a good day. But she was curvy everywhere else.

Especially her hips and ass.

She was one of those people who looked better naked than in clothes. Clothing just didn't always fit correctly and didn't show off her assets.

Naked, or nearly naked, was much better.

He'd seen her in the bikini twice. Once in the pool yesterday morning, but half of her was covered by water, and again when she'd pulled the wetsuit on and off, but it had been quick and he'd been dealing with his own. This was different. This was her standing in front of him, showing him her body. Asking him to look.

His eyes devoured her, raking over every inch of skin. "Fuck me, you're gorgeous." He reached out, skimming a hand down her side, sending chills through her whole body with just that small touch. "There are so many things I want to do to you. With you."

"Then you better get started." She was goading him, but he wasn't the only one who was on edge. She wanted this man. Badly. She liked how he made her feel: strong and invincible.

He pressed his body against her once again, trailing his lips over the skin on her shoulder until he reached her ear. "I'll go as slow or as fast as I want, and you'll just have to deal with it."

A shiver raced through her again at his words. She didn't like dominant men as a rule, but with Alec, it was a completely different story. She not only enjoyed it, but sort of craved it.

His mouth was on hers, kissing her as his hands roamed freely over her body. She practically purred when he cupped her breasts, running his thumbs over her nipples through the fabric of her bikini. She arched her body against his, telling him without words what she wanted.

His hands moved around her body to her back as he unclasped the swimsuit top effortlessly. It fell between their bodies, as he lowered his head, kissing his way down her chest until he reached a breast. He teased her nipple once, twice with his tongue before his lips circled it, sucking it forcefully.

She bellowed loudly. "Ahhhh!" His mouth continued to

tease her nipple until she was squirming and begging him to stop.

"Is that what you really want?" His head was lifted just enough for her to see his eyes as he asked the question. "For me to stop?"

"Yes. No. I don't fucking know." She gripped his head. "It's too good."

He grinned before lowering his head once again and grazing her nipple with his lips. "No such thing."

Maybe he was right. It might be too good, but she wasn't ready for it to end. Needing just a little control, she pushed on his shoulders to get him moving just a little faster.

He got the message and kissed his way down her body until he was on his knees in front of her.

Was there anything hotter than a guy kneeling at your feet, ready to eat your pussy?

She didn't think so.

The look on his face as he lowered her bikini bottoms told her he felt the same way. There was nowhere else he'd rather be.

"You're fucking drenched," he said with his face so close to the promised land but not actually touching her with his mouth.

If she had a camera on her, this was a photo she'd like to have to remember this exact moment. She spread her legs a little more, hoping he got the hint. "I believe that is your fault."

His hands trailed up her legs until his thumbs finally grazed over her damp pussy. She jumped at the slight contact, moaning out. "So responsive," he murmured, and then before she had any warning whatsoever, he leaned in, swiping his tongue through her folds.

The sound that came from her was one of pure animalistic need.

She needed this man. Needed him to make her come, needed him to soothe her, and needed him to fuck her.

She was sort of afraid that need would become so much more once he did all those things.

Chapter Nine

Alec

There were moments in your life that you wanted to forget and moments that you hoped you'd remember forever.

This was one he wanted to remember in exact detail until the day he died.

The sounds she made, the way her body was dripping for him, and the need in her eyes were all part of what made this the perfect moment. If he could live right here, in this exact moment, for the rest of his life, he'd be happy.

That thought scared the shit out of him.

From the moment he'd laid eyes on Penny in the pool, he'd been infatuated to the point of obsession. He'd never looked at someone and needed them that way. Meeting her, talking to her, kissing her, surfing with her, all those things, only dug the hole deeper.

He had a feeling that even if she lived in another town,

he'd have uprooted his life to have her in it. A scary thought indeed.

"Alec, please," she begged, her body quivering with need.

Who was he to deny her pleasure?

He changed from soft licks to opening his mouth wider and devouring her. He speared her with his tongue, alternating between licking and fucking. When it wasn't enough, he grabbed hold of her leg, lifting it over his shoulder, opening her up to him even more. She was wet, and getting wetter by the second so when he slipped his fingers through her folds and into her body, they went in easily.

"Oh God," she moaned, pressing herself even harder against his face, searching for her release.

He fucked her hard with two fingers, his tongue flicking her clit over and over.

On a whim, he held his fingers inside her, hooking them just a little. His whim paid off when she detonated, coming hard all over his face.

"Holy shit. Holy shit. Holy shit," she mumbled over and over.

The same words were repeating in his head. He knew what squirting was and had even made a woman do it once before. But he'd never attempted it while his face was plastered against a pussy. He'd never wanted to. He'd tried it with Penny without a thought as to what would happen if he actually succeeded.

The outcome exceeded anything he knew about women and orgasms and what he liked and didn't like.

He wasn't grossed out. It was the opposite. The way she'd come and released juices all over his face turned him on in a way he'd never even known existed.

"Alec," she said, her voice heady with desire.

He helped her lower her leg to the ground, and then before she could protest, he picked her up in his arms, carrying her to the bed. He laid her down gently, before stripping off his clothes as she watched with hooded eyes. His dick was hard and ready as he gave it several strokes while she watched.

There was something amazing about having her eyes on him.

"You're so fucking sexy," he told her as he tore open the condom he'd placed on his nightstand earlier in the hopes that something like this would happen.

Although, in his wildest dreams, he'd never imagined what had just happened.

"Was that..." she trailed off, biting down on her bottom lip. With the condom on, he leaned over her on the bed, pulling her lip from her mouth with his thumb.

"Don't bite this lip, baby." He touched his lips to hers, sucking her bottom lip into his mouth, biting it just enough to have her eyes widening. "Now, ask your question."

His face was still covered in her release since he hadn't bothered to wipe it off. He knew she could taste herself on him.

"That's never happened to me while someone's face was down there."

He felt ten feet tall at her admission. "Lucky me."

"It didn't turn you off?" Her eyes showed confusion.

To show her just how much it didn't turn him off, he pressed his dick against her leg. "Does this answer your question? It was hot and totally unexpected but not at all a turn off. If anything, it might have made me want you more." He wasn't sure how that was possible since he already wanted her more than he'd ever wanted another woman. And that included the girl he'd lost his virginity to, Betty Roy, when he was seventeen and only thought of sex.

"Then what are you waiting for?" She raised her eyebrows in question and, in a move that told him she knew what she was doing, bit down on her bottom lip again.

His control snapped if he'd ever even had any. He leaned forward again, whispering, "What did I tell you about biting this lip." Then because he could, he pulled it from her mouth with his own teeth.

Her seductive moan told him she was ready for everything he had to give.

Snaking his hand between them as he continued to kiss her passionately, he pressed the head of his dick against her opening. They moaned together at the feeling and that drove him over the edge. With one hard thrust, he was seated fully inside her.

Her body gripped him tightly as he tried to breathe through the desire to come instantly. That's how good being inside her felt.

"Alec," she said his name in a whispered desperation.

He knew just how she felt.

"Tell me if this is too much." He started slowly thrusting in and out, praying to anyone that would listen to make him last long enough to make her come.

"It's not too much." Her hands were around his neck, her nails digging into his back. "More, give me more," Her broken words and needy voice had him thrusting harder.

Wanting to be deeper, to feel more of her wrapped around him, he sat back, lifting her legs and pushing them toward her chest. Not only did this make it easier to control how deep he went, but he was able to watch his cock disappear inside her gorgeous pussy.

In his mind, there was no better view.

Her hand dipped between her legs, her fingers coming into contact with her clit.

If possible, watching her find her pleasure made him harder. "That's it, play with your clit. Make yourself come all over my cock." His voice was harsh in a way he'd never sounded before.

Penny turned him into a different guy. Normally, he was a guy who was organized and thought things through. He was kind and helpful. The guy that was fucking her and telling her to make herself come was someone else entirely.

He wasn't sure he hated him.

If being a little demanding got him balls deep inside the hottest woman he'd ever met, he wasn't sure that was a bad thing.

"Alec, oh god." Her eyes closed, and he knew from the way she was panting and how she arched into him that she was there.

He pounded into her harder and watched as she came apart under him. It was glorious and sexy and more than he'd ever known was possible. The way her body shook and convulsed with pleasure had his own orgasm barrelling through him without warning.

Penny's eyes opened at his deep groan, and she held his gaze as he pumped furiously into her body. When he was finished, both his mind and body were overtaken with so much exhaustion that he went limp on top of her.

In his euphoric haze, he felt her hands trailing up and down his back.

"I should move," he said, his voice raspy.

"Not yet," she said, gripping him tightly. "I like the way you feel on top of me."

He lifted his head, wanting to see her face. "I like the way I feel on top of you too."

She rolled her eyes, a smile on her lips. "Don't be an ass."

"I really do need to move, though. Condom and all." He knew it wasn't the sexiest conversation, but a leaky condom after their first time together wouldn't be good.

She sighed in reluctance. "You're probably right." She loosened her grip, allowing him to roll off her.

After quickly taking care of the condom, he laid down next to her. "So that was unexpected." He turned his head to take her in. Her hair was messy, and she had the cutest red blotches on her face from the exertion.

Even a mess, she was gorgeous.

She turned to her side, facing him. "Was it really unexpected?" She raised an eyebrow. "Because if I'm being honest, I'm surprised we held out this long."

He couldn't stop the laugh that bubbled out of him. "Not unexpected as in I didn't think it was going to happen. Because, let's be real, you're right, it was always going to happen. It's more how it came to be that was unexpected. I never thought surfing would be the way to your heart."

She lifted her head, propping it up on a hand. "The second I saw you at the pool holding that surfboard, it was a foregone conclusion that we'd end up here. The surfboard may have grabbed my attention, but it was you who held it." Her free hand landed on his chest, her fingers toying with the hair there.

His heartbeat sped up in his chest at her confession. He'd felt the same way when he'd spotted her in the pool. His heart had stopped and then beat frantically in his chest.

It was like nothing he'd ever experienced. He'd said many things to her in the last day that he probably should have kept to himself. He needed to play it cool if he had any chance of not scaring her away.

To break the tension and make sure he kept his mouth shut, he pulled her on top of him, her legs easily straddling his waist as she sat up. Her tits were right there, and because he loved them, he cupped each one, running his thumbs over her nipples.

She moaned, so he kept doing it.

"Alec." Hearing his name coming out of her mouth, breathy and needy, was his new favorite thing. Well, right behind her coming around his cock.

That would top his list for the rest of his life.

"Tell me what you want." He wanted to hear her thoughts, all her dirty, wicked thoughts.

She held his gaze as she slid backward, taking her tits away from his hands. "I want to suck your cock." The words were said with such conviction and want that his dick went from half hard to fully hard in an instant.

There were guys who loved blow jobs and guys who hated them. He sat somewhere in the middle. They were fine and had been good enough to get him off in his younger years, but these days, it took more than a dick-sucking to make him come.

How did you classily tell someone that they most likely wouldn't make you come?

Just as he was about to open his mouth and mention it, her tongue licked the head of his dick, and every previous thought he had about blowjobs went out the window. That one touch from her tongue felt better than anything anyone else had ever done.

Maybe it wasn't the act of a blow job he hated, but who was giving it to him.

Her hand gripped him at the base as she licked him again and then smiled. "God, I love dicks."

He choked out a laugh. "Good to know." Was he hyperventilating? It sure as shit felt like it.

"No, I don't think you understand what I'm saying." She twirled her tongue around the tip of his dick, her tongue toying with the hole.

He had to grip the covers to stop himself from grabbing her head and fucking her mouth.

"I really love dick. And yours is pretty fucking phenomenal." She sat up just a little, looking down at his dick. "I mean, really, who needs this much? The length is good and all, but the width is a little ridiculous. I'm not even sure I can fit it fully in my mouth." She stroked him up and down in her fist as she talked. A fist that didn't quite fit all the way around his dick.

Somehow, that made him smile. If her hand couldn't fit around him, how was she ever going to take him in her mouth?

He liked the thought of her struggling to suck him off.

Did that make him perverse? Probably, but he didn't care.

"Are you going to suck my dick or talk about it?" He suddenly wanted nothing more than this woman's mouth around his dick. He could picture himself coming hard down her throat, and that thought alone had him halfway to orgasm.

She winked, leaning forward again and once again licking the underside of his dick. "I'm savoring this. Who knows when I'll get to do it again."

If she wanted to suck his dick every day, he'd let her. Ten minutes ago, he'd have never thought that. A few touches of her tongue to his dick, and he'd quickly changed his mind.

He was apparently going to be one of those guys who said their girlfriend's mouth was magic.

Shit, he'd just thought of her as his girlfriend. He had to slow his roll. She was a woman he was sleeping with. One he wanted to sleep with again. Multiple times. She was in no way his girlfriend.

Not yet.

Chapter Ten

Penny

The man had a nice dick, that was without question. The part she was questioning was whether or not she could suck it without getting a locked jaw. She'd never had one so thick. It was seriously like a soda can. Maybe just a little smaller.

Or maybe not.

When it had been inside her, she'd been too caught up in how amazing it had felt to think about the girth. Although it explained why she'd had no trouble orgasming. For her, girth was the key. Length did nothing for her.

That was another thing that was going to make keeping this casual difficult. No one's dick was ever perfect.

Alec's was.

Her hand gripped him tightly and he swore. "Penny." Her name was a curse and she loved that she made him that way.

"Is there something you wanted?" She lowered her face but didn't put her mouth on him.

"Suck my fucking cock." He sounded as if he was in pain.

She couldn't have that.

Without any more teasing, she closed her mouth around the head of his dick and the sound he made had her squeezing her thighs together for relief.

The man made the best noises.

She focused on the task at hand as she bobbed up and down on his dick. It wasn't easy to hold her mouth open that wide for long periods of time so she alternated between sucking him and licking around the head with her tongue.

If the noises and grunts and groans of her name were any indication, he didn't seem to mind. She kept up the pace, taking him deeper each time until the head hit the back of her throat.

"Penny," he moaned as his hands landed on her head, his fingers tangling in her hair.

Finally. She'd felt him struggling for control but she'd wanted his hands in her hair. She wanted him to lift his hips and fuck her mouth.

She flicked her eyes to his as her mouth was wrapped widely around his shaft, telling him with her eyes that this was okay, that it was what she wanted.

"Goddamn, your mouth looks good around my cock."

She shivered at his words, wishing she had the dexterity to slip her free hand between her legs and stroke her clit. She was pretty sure if she tried that, she'd somehow fall off the bed.

His grip tightened in her hair and she groaned around

his dick at the sensation. "That's it. Keep sucking. You're going to make me come."

He sounded sort of shocked at that, but really, wasn't that the whole point?

He was murmuring words about not believing this was real and how good her mouth felt but she was in a daze. A dick daze. All she cared about was finishing what she started and making him feel good. He'd made her feel better than anyone before, and she wanted the same thing for him.

She knew it was a long shot. There were surely women out there who sucked cock better, but she was going to give it the old college try. Someone might be better, but it was hard to believe there were many women who loved doing this as much as she did.

From conversations with friends, she knew she was unique in that area.

She relaxed her jaw even more as she worked his cock. He was a puddle of mess and incoherent words, and she loved it. She'd made him that way.

"Penny, I'm coming," he groaned.

This was the moment she'd been waiting for. His release. When she'd been younger, she'd shied away from guys coming in her mouth. To this day, she rarely allowed it. But with Alec, she wanted it. She wanted everything he had to give her.

She sucked him deep, his release hitting her mouth and throat as she swallowed it as quickly as she could. When she felt him go placid under her, she sat back, licking her lips, a smile on her face.

"Fuck me," he swore, his voice gravelly.

She laughed. "Like that, did you?"

He gripped her around the waist, pulling her until she

was lying on top of him and his lips were on hers. "It was incredible." He kissed her, desperate at first, but then it slowed and became gentle and all she could think was this was how kisses were supposed to be.

"Want to hear a confession?" he asked, his lips trailing over her face, kissing her everywhere.

"I love a good confession."

"I haven't come from a blow job in years."

She stilled, her eyes going wide. Sitting up, she looked down at him. "What? How is that possible?"

He looked a little sheepish as he said, "It just stopped feeling good a while ago, and I couldn't come that way."

She was unsure what to say to his confession. It made her feel proud in an odd sort of way to be the person who made him like a good dick-sucking. But, it was also just a little bit scary, if she was being honest with herself.

She was getting in too deep with someone who she should probably keep it more casual with.

"I'm happy to show you the error of your ways. Now you know they feel good." She was trying for light and silly as she rolled off him.

He sat up, leaning over her. "Penny." He closed his eyes and swore under his breath. When he opened his eyes back up, she saw so much emotion. "Let's just say I don't think I'd come like that from anyone else giving me a blow job."

She got the sense that he wanted to say more, but instead, he fell back down next to her, sighing loudly.

She was so happy, so content that there wasn't a need to fill the silence in the room with talking. That had never been the case before. It made her wonder why this was different. Why was he so different?

A loud bang on the door interrupted her thoughts and had Alec groaning.

"If that is one of my friends, you're going to have to bail me out of a Mexican jail for murder." He stood up from the bed, grabbing a pair of shorts from a nearby chair. While he did that, she pulled the covers up over herself even though you couldn't see the bed from the door.

The banging continued and sounded like more than one person.

"What the fuck," Alec said as she heard him pull open the door.

"What took you so long?" a voice said, and if Penny had to guess, it was JT.

"Why are you assholes banging on my door?" Alec asked.

"Penny wouldn't happen to be with you, would she?" That was definitely Gabe who asked the question.

"So what if she is?" Alec asked.

"Hey, man, I don't care, but her friends are looking for her and apparently her phone is off."

Shit. Penny totally forgot that she turned her phone off before going surfing with Alec and hadn't given it a thought since. Grabbing the comforter and wrapping it around her, she got off the bed and went to the door.

"Hey, guys, tell my friends I'll call them in a little." She bent down, grabbing her small bag from the floor where she'd dropped it when they'd walked in.

"Hey, Penny," JT said. "Nice to see you again." He winked at her with a huge grin on his face.

"Asshole, stop winking at her." Alec pushed him out of the doorway and back out into the hallway. "You have your proof that she's fine." As he closed the door, Penny could hear JT laughing.

Alec turned to face her. "You're naked."

She looked down at the comforter that covered her entire body. "This covers more of me than my bikini."

He moved toward her, forcing her back against the wall and grabbing the material of the comforter in his fist, pulling it from her body. "Except in your bikini, you don't look freshly fucked."

His eyes were dark and his intention was clear. He was going to fuck her against the wall.

And she was going to love it.

"You're only wearing shorts." She ran her fingers down his chest to his stomach. "Why is that different?" She was goading him once again and she knew it. So did he from the expression on his face.

"Because I don't want my friends to see you like this." He pressed his body against hers, gripping her head in his large hand and sealing his mouth against hers. The kiss was punishing but she loved it. His jealousy somehow spurred her on in a way that jealousy never had before.

Her fingers dug into his shoulders, holding him close, wanting him even closer. She loved the feel of his naked skin beneath her hands and wished she never had to let go.

A scary thought if there ever was one.

"Don't fucking move," he said when he tore his mouth away from hers. She leaned her head against the wall and watched as he moved quickly across the room grabbing what she could only assume was a condom. He stripped off his shorts as he made his way back to her, his cock already hard against his stomach.

She licked her lips in anticipation of what was to come.

"Fuck, don't do that or I'll make you get on your knees and suck me off again."

Why was the thought of him making her get on her knees so hot? "Aren't you the same guy who just admitted to not loving blow jobs?"

He tore open the condom, sliding it down his hard dick. "That was before. Now that I know what your mouth feels like wrapped around my dick, I'm back to liking them." With the condom on, he pressed his body up against hers, his cock slipping easily between her legs. "But I think I like this better."

Yeah, so did she.

Chapter Eleven

Alec

The smile on his face was bigger than it had ever been. And that was all thanks to Penny.

It wasn't just the sex, although that was fucking fantastic. It was her. She was funny and goofy and smart and sexy. She was basically perfect. Who met the perfect person on vacation?

Apparently, he did.

The question was, what was he going to do about it?

"You know, she won't disappear if you stop looking at her for two seconds." Beside him, he heard Gabe's voice but didn't look over. Penny might not disappear, but he liked looking at her.

"You're fucking hysterical."

They were all at the pool, all eight of them, and the girls were in the water laughing about something with drinks in their hands while he and his friends sat in chairs watching.

At least he was watching. He didn't know what the other guys were doing.

"I've never seen him like this," JT said. "Should we call a doctor?"

"Leave him alone," Ben said.

"You only say that because you are staring at Annabelle the same way he's staring at Penny," Gabe said.

"Fuck off," Ben said.

"Whoa," Gabe said, and Alec turned to look at Ben.

Ben was known for falling for women quickly, but Alec had never seen him get aggressive over one.

"Is this more than just a fling?" he asked.

Ben groaned, pushing his sunglasses on top of his head. "I don't fucking know. Annabelle says that we had fun and that she enjoyed our night together, but that's it. I don't know how to take that. Does she want to see me when we leave here? Was this a one-night thing?"

"I have an idea," JT said. "Ask her."

"What if the answer isn't the one I'm looking for?" Ben leaned back in his lounger, closing his eyes.

That was the same question Alec wanted the answer to. He badly wanted to see Penny again, but what if this was just a fun vacation fling for her?

"I guess the rumors are true," Gabe said. "Sex makes you stupid."

Alec couldn't help but laugh at that statement. He'd definitely felt like his brain had melted after his morning with Penny. They'd meshed together so well after only knowing each other less than a day. That had never been the case before.

It had to mean more than just a vacation fling.

"Alec, please tell me you aren't as dumb as Ben over here." Gabe said. "You don't fall for the vacation pussy."

"When you get vacation pussy, you can talk," Alec said. "Until then, maybe be helpful instead of an asshole."

JT laughed loudly. "He's got you there."

Gabe flipped JT off and then said, "Fine, but if you two are going to be all googly eyes over women, I'm going to get another drink." He stood up and walked away.

Alec leaned back in his lounger, his eyes once again searching out Penny. As soon as he locked eyes on her, she turned her head, giving him a small smile and a wave. His dick went instantly hard.

Swim trunks were not optimal for hard ons.

"I can't believe we have to go back to cold Ohio tomorrow," Gabe said. "This was like a tease for summer when we still have a couple of months to go before it's consistently warm."

"I plan not to leave my house during those months," JT said. "Winter and spring are for gaming."

"You say that every year, and yet every time I ask if you wanna play, you allegedly have plans." Ben removed his sunglasses, sitting forward.

"It's not my fault I have a life outside you assholes," JT said.

"Hooking up with a woman you just met and then never seeing her again is not a quality social life," Alec said. "And wasn't it just you on the flight down here who told me he was sick of that life?" Alec pretended to look around. "Or was that someone else?"

JT groaned. "I can't believe I blabbed that to you. For the record, I'm not sick of sex. I'm sick of meaningless sex."

"I'm sure those women you conned into sex are also sick

of it too." A woman's voice entered the conversation, and they all looked up to see Mya standing in front of them.

"I don't have to con women into sex," JT snapped. "For your information, I have women throwing themselves at me."

"As evident by all the women surrounding you." Mya smiled wickedly, knowing she'd just won that round.

"Have we switched places?" Jodi stepped up next to Mya. "Is this a Freaky Friday thing? Because usually I'm the ball buster, and you are sweet and nice."

"I'm trying something new." Mya shrugged like it was no big deal.

"What are we talking about?" Annabelle said, as she and Penny joined the group. Annabelle plopped down on Ben's chair easily like it was the most normal thing to do.

Alec watched Penny closely, wondering if she was going to do the same, only on his chair. She glanced at him, almost like she was thinking about it. But instead of sitting on his chair, she sat down on the edge of the pool right in front of them, putting her feet in the water. Mya followed suit, and Jodi, being who she was, sat down on the edge of JT's chair.

"I hate that we have to go home tomorrow," Penny said, turning back to look directly at him. "This has been the best vacation."

"I vote no more weekend shopping trips or cabins," Annabelle said. "We should always come to the beach for our yearly getaway."

"Agreed," Mya said.

"You guys say that like it's so easy to coordinate," Jodi added. "Do you know how hard it was to find five days that worked for all of us?"

"If anyone can do it, you can," Penny said, pumping her friend up.

Alec and the guys just sat and listened to them chat and bicker, adding to the conversation, if warranted. There was more drinking and more swimming, and more laughter. He couldn't think of a better way to spend his last day in paradise.

Well, he could think of one. And it involved his body wrapped around Penny's as she moaned his name.

They decided to have dinner together as a group, and Jodi somehow used her powers of persuasion to sweet-talk one of the restaurants into seating them as a party of eight. When they parted ways to go get ready for dinner, Penny grabbed his arm, holding him back.

He took the opportunity to touch her, placing his hand on her hip. "Did you need something?"

"I was thinking," she bit down on her bottom lip, "maybe we could conserve water and shower together?"

The fact that she was acting innocent after the things they'd done together turned him on in a way he hadn't known existed. "That depends," he said, joining in on her game, "does shower mean get clean or get dirty?"

Heat flared in her eyes. "Dirty. Definitely dirty."

He closed the distance between them, unable to go even one more second without kissing her. The kiss was explosive, both of them reaching for the other, searching for anything to grip onto.

"I'll grab my stuff and meet you in your room," he said when he was able to drag his lips from hers.

"Hurry," she said, her eyes filled with even more heat than before.

He should probably tell someone they would be late for dinner. But that was the last thing on his mind as he jogged the pathways toward his room. Once there, he grabbed his backpack and shoved some clothes and a few essentials inside. He was only in his room a matter of minutes before heading out and once again jogging the paths. The sooner he got to Penny's room, the sooner he got to see her naked.

And seeing her naked was like seeing God.

She was fucking gorgeous.

He reached her door and was about to knock when it flew open and she pulled him inside.

"What took you so long?"

The thud of his bag hitting the floor was loud as he pulled Penny into his arms and latched his lips with hers. He'd kissed her many times during their time together that morning, but throughout the day, when they'd been with their friends, he'd somehow held himself back.

It had been torture.

Kissing her was now one of his favorite things.

And he wasn't just talking about kissing her lips. Every part of her deserved to be kissed. Not only that, but he loved kissing her everywhere. Her skin was soft, and she made the sweetest sounds as his lips moved across her body.

"Get naked," she said breathlessly as she tried pushing his trunks down. "All day, all I've thought about was you naked and inside me. I can't wait."

Who was he to make her wait when he wanted the exact same thing?

Together they stripped off what minimal clothes they had on since they were both still in swimwear, and after Penny handed him a condom, he made quick work of rolling it on before she pushed him down onto the chair in the corner.

He looked up at her, his hand fisting around his dick, stroking it up and down. "I see someone wants to be on top."

"Damn straight," She climbed onto his lap, easily sliding down on his cock with how wet she was. "Fuck, that feels good."

He was in agreement but couldn't speak because of how fucking good it felt. He was deathly afraid that if he opened his mouth, he'd confess his undying love for her when he wasn't even sure if he was in love with her.

That's how good her pussy felt wrapped around his cock. It made him want to do things he'd never done before.

Like confess love.

His fingers gripped her hips as she moved up and down on his cock, taking him along for the ride of a lifetime. Her head was thrown back in ecstasy, and she moaned and murmured about how good his cock felt and how much she'd missed it.

Wait. She didn't say *it*, she said *him*.

She'd missed him. Not just some faceless guy whose dick she liked. She specifically liked his dick.

His fingers on her hips tightened as he decided it was time for him to be in control. "You need to come?" His words were gruff and crude, but the way her body contracted around his cock told him she liked it.

"Please, yes, please, make me come." Her words were broken and choppy but full of so much need.

He toyed with the idea of slowing down, making her wait. But his body wanted its own release, and there was no way he could hold back. He held her down, furiously pumping his hips, giving her the most friction right where she needed it.

"Harder," she begged.

He wasn't sure how much harder he could fuck her, but if she wanted it harder, he'd give it to her. Planting his feet wide on the floor, he leaned forward, pulling her against his chest as his hips continued to pound into her. He felt her fingers claw against the skin of his neck and back, which only spurred him on more.

He wanted the marks she was leaving. Craved them, really. When he went home the next day, he wanted this reminder of their time together.

"Your pussy feels so amazing," he said as he continued to fuck her. "You gotta come, baby." His own release was so close. But there was no way he was going over without her.

"I'm there, I'm there, I'm there," she chanted over and over until her body tensed, and she threw her head back, letting out a long groan.

He finally gave in to his own body and came right behind her, holding her tightly to his chest as he closed his eyes and relished having her in his arms.

"Holy moly," she said, her words muffled since her face was plastered against his neck.

He gave himself a few seconds to slow his breathing before loosening his hold on her and leaning back in the chair. He looked her up and down, from her face to where their bodies were connected. Seeing his dick inside her had him growing hard again.

"I thought you brought me here to shower?" he quipped.

"That's next," she said, standing up, his hard cock sticking straight up and ready for more. "This was just a warm-up."

He didn't need to be told twice that there was more sex waiting. He was no dummy.

Chapter Twelve

Penny

Shower sex was not all it was cracked up to be.

Unless it was with Alec.

Apparently, the man had shower sex skills that other men, at least in her experience, did not have.

One example is the way he got down on his knees on the hard tile floor and licked her pussy until she came.

Skills.

Mad fucking skills.

She returned the favor, sort of, by jerking him off. Her knees might only be twenty-five years old, but they were not meant for kneeling on hard tile. Plus, he didn't complain. In fact, he came so fast and so hard, which told her he didn't mind in the least.

It could have also been the dirty words she was whispering in his ear as she jerked him off. He really seemed to like those.

"I should text and let the guys know we're going to be late," Alec said as he dried himself off with a towel.

"Already done," she said. "I texted Mya before you got here to let her know."

He came to stand behind her, where she was applying lotion to her arms. His head lowered to her ear. "Well in that case..." His tongue toyed with her ear before biting down.

She moaned at how good it felt. "You tempt me, that's for sure." She turned in his arms. "But we promised our friends." Turning down sex, good sex, sex that she might never get to have again, for her friends, was huge. They were going to owe her.

He groaned. "I hate it when you're right." He smacked his lips against hers in a quick kiss but then stepped back.

"Which is always," she said, hoping it came out as it was meant—cutely and jokingly—as she went back to applying lotion.

"Something tells me that's a true statement," Alec said as he walked out of the bathroom.

She exhaled deeply now that he was out of the room. This was getting messy. She liked him. A lot. And not just the sex, although that was fucking phenomenal. She liked him as a person. In the day they'd spent together, she'd learned that he was funny and smart and generous. Many times, he volunteered to get drinks or grab something for someone. He'd even gone to the pizza place at the resort and picked up a couple of pizzas for them all to munch on throughout the day.

This wasn't supposed to happen. She wasn't supposed to come on vacation and meet the perfect guy.

The perfect guy who just happened to live where she lived.

If she didn't know any better, she'd say her mom had made a deal with the devil for her to find a guy. One of the reasons she never told her mom anything about her dating life. She'd get attached and be planning a wedding while Penny was just in it for fun.

Sometimes, she wished she had the relationship Mya had with her mom. They talked about everything, and Mya told her mom every detail of her dating and sex life. Well, not every detail. She left out specifics about sex.

"Gabe is texting asking how long we think we're going to be," Alec shouted from the bedroom.

"I can be ready in five minutes."

Alec's head peeked around the corner, his expression curious. "Is that a real five minutes or a football five minutes?"

She laughed. Having watched a lot of football in her life, she knew just what he was talking about. "Real. I just have to throw on a splash of eyeliner and mascara and get dressed." She'd let her hair air dry, saving fifteen minutes.

"You could always stay naked, and we could tell our friends to go ahead and eat without us." He stepped into the bathroom, skimming his hand down her side and then across her naked ass.

"Tempting, but you're already dressed and if I do say so myself, looking pretty hot." He was in navy blue shorts with a white button-down shirt with the sleeves rolled up.

Rolled sleeves were her kryptonite.

Why were forearms so sexy? The corded muscles and splash of hair. It was just too much.

He leaned against the sink, watching her as she put on her mascara. It made her nervous in a way to have him watching so intently, but it also made her hot and horny.

They needed to leave the room before she took him up on his offer, and they never left.

After setting her mascara tube down, she turned, brushing her naked breasts against his side as she walked past him.

"You're such a tease!" he shouted a few seconds after she'd passed.

She laughed as she found a simple summer dress and pulled it on. Alec stepped out of the bathroom just in time to see it cover her body.

"Did you put underwear on?" He raised an eyebrow.

She patted the dress, pretending to feel around. "You know, I must have forgotten." She shrugged playfully. "Oops."

He groaned loudly. "If I fuck you in public, just know you brought it on yourself."

She laughed as she grabbed her small purse and phone. "Maybe I'd be okay with that." She wasn't sure she would, but she had to keep up her front of liking naughty things. Which wasn't really a front at all because she did like naughty things. Especially when they came from him.

Alec shook his head as he opened the door for her. When she started to walk through, he stopped her with a hand on her hip. "Next time I fuck you, it will be in private, where I can have you naked and screaming my name."

She sucked in a breath at his words, wanting precisely what he said.

Dinner. Friends. They had to meet their friends for dinner. Sex could happen later.

Hopefully, not too much later. She had to leave the hotel somewhat early to make it to the airport for her flight. That made her wonder when his flight was. Surely there was no way they were on the same flight.

"What time is your flight tomorrow?" she asked as they walked toward the center of the resort where the restaurants were located.

"Eleven. What about you?"

She stopped walking and doubled over in laughter. Because now she knew the universe or something like it was fucking with her.

"I take it you are on the same flight?" It was ridiculous how easily he'd learned to read her in just a day.

She stood up, her laughter still echoing into the night. "What are the odds?"

"I mean, we are going to the exact same city, so I'd say pretty good." He was taking this all in stride, and she wasn't sure what that meant. Was it because he never planned to see her again? Sure, he'd said he'd wanted to but people said lots of things when they wanted sex or to keep having sex. Maybe it was all an act.

"Do you guys have transport to the airport lined up?" he asked as they walked.

"We had a private transfer coming here, so I assume that's how we're leaving. Jodi is in charge and we just trust her."

"Since we stayed a day longer than the rest of our company, we were responsible for our own transportation. Gabe got us squared away, but like you, I didn't question it. Do you know your seat number?"

She pulled her phone out from her purse and swiped until she found the airline app. "Twelve D."

He had his own phone out, also looking. "I'm twenty-nine A." He looked at her as they continued to walk. "Maybe I can sweet talk one of your friends into switching with me."

"Since it's Jodi sitting next to me, I'm going to say that's highly unlikely." While Jodi didn't fully think this thing with Alec was a bad idea, she wasn't one hundred percent on board either.

"Well, Gabe is next to me and he owes me, so if you'd like to spend three hours with me cramped on a plane, I can make it happen."

She had no idea how to answer that. Of course, she wanted to spend as much time with him as possible but what if this was it and they never saw each other again? Hell, she didn't even have his phone number. "Let's see how tonight goes," she said, hoping that sufficed as a good enough answer.

He gave her an odd look but then looked straight ahead again. "Yeah, that's cool."

His words were clipped, almost as if he were mad or annoyed.

Ugh, she hated trying to read minds. But she didn't know him well enough to know his moods or tones. That was the problem. They'd just met, and she was all in her head planning a future when this could fizzle out in weeks or even days.

She was going to play it cool and see what happened.

Not something she was good at but there was a first for everything.

When they entered the restaurant, they spotted their group immediately, in part because they were towards the front but also because they were loud. She was used to both Jodi and Mya being loud but was shocked to hear Annabelle's voice over everyone else's.

"Hey," she said as they approached the table.

"About time," JT said. "Some of us are hungry."

"If I had to guess, Alec already had dessert," Mya said with a smirk.

"Ugh, don't put that image in my head." Ben cringed.

"I won't confirm or deny that comment," Alec said, pulling out one of the two remaining chairs for her.

"That just leaves you, Pen," Jodi said. "Care to comment?"

Penny looked at Alec and decided what the hell, they were all friends. "He did have a snack recently."

Laughter and taunts went up around the table. Alec leaned in, whispering in her ear. "A snack? I'm pretty sure that was a full meal. And it was delicious."

His words had her pressing her thighs together for some relief. Maybe no underwear was a bad idea.

On her other side, Mya nudged her shoulder. "Way to get yours."

She stayed silent, because really what could she say? She'd loved every minute of it and wanted to do it all again. Every day.

"Ben was telling me that they are on the same flight as us tomorrow," Annabelle said. "How crazy is that?"

"Not that crazy," Alec said under his breath.

She looked at him, wondering why he sounded annoyed. Or maybe he didn't sound annoyed. How was she supposed to know?

"Mya, do you think you can switch seats with Ben so we can sit next to each other?" Annabelle gave a sad puppy dog face, one that none of them could ignore.

"Fine," Mya said. "Who am I sitting by?"

"Me," JT said quietly, barely audible over the noise surrounding them.

Mya's expression started to change but she caught herself and smiled before anyone else caught it, but Penny saw it. Mya was usually friendly with everyone but for some reason, she had an attitude when it came to JT.

That was something she was going to question her friend about once they were home.

"I suppose that means you want me to switch with Penny," Gabe said, looking at Alec.

"That's up to Penny," Alec said, his voice void of emotion.

"Really," Jodi said. "I planned this whole trip and now I have to sit next to him?" She pointed to Gabe with her thumb. "That's the thanks I get."

"What's wrong with me?" Gabe asked with frustration.

"You're cocky and I don't like it."

"I'm cocky?" he said like it was news to him. "Pot meet kettle."

"Guys," Penny said to calm everyone down before it went too far. "It's fine. No one has to switch seats."

Beside her, she felt Alec stiffen before pushing his chair back. "I'm gonna go to the bar to grab a drink."

"I'll go with you," JT said.

"Me too," both Ben and Gabe said at the same time.

When all the guys were gone, her friends all spoke at the same time.

"What was that?" Mya said.

"Are you crazy?" Annabelle said.

"Is this fling over already?" Jodi said.

She decided to answer them all.

"No I'm not crazy, I don't know what that was, and fuck if I know." She badly needed her own drink and was sort of surprised that Alec hadn't asked what she wanted.

"Okay, we're going to need more," Jodi said. "You guys obviously had sex before coming here so what happened between then and now?"

"If I knew that, Alec wouldn't have just left the table."

"You don't think it has anything to do with you saying you don't want to sit with him on the way home?" Annabelle asked, raising one eyebrow perfectly.

"That's not what I said. I was just defusing the situation between Jodi and Gabe by saying no one had to switch seats."

"That might be what you were doing but I don't think that's how he took it," Mya said. "Granted I don't know him as well as you do but he seemed pissed."

"Fucking great." She threw her hands up. "This is why dating sucks. Keeping it at sex is a much better option."

Even as she said the words, she knew they weren't true. She didn't want just sex from Alec. She liked him and would like to see where this could lead. But how could she do that when at every corner, she was fucking it up?

As much as it would suck, maybe she just needed to pull the plug and stop whatever this was before it went any further.

Chapter Thirteen

Alec

The anger inside him at how easily Penny had dismissed sitting next to him on the plane was easily more anger than he could ever remember feeling.

Even worse than when he didn't make the varsity soccer team in high school, but the coach's son, who was not nearly as good as him, did.

"Tequila," he said to the bartender a little too harshly.

"Dude," JT said, coming up beside him, "you need to calm down."

"If you only followed me to give me advice I can get from a Taylor Swift song, you can leave."

"Dude," Gabe said, flanking his other side, "we followed you because you're blowing it with a woman you really seem to like."

"I'm blowing it? You heard what she said." The bartender pushed his shot of tequila toward him, and he grabbed it, throwing it back quickly. It burned, but in a good way.

"She was obviously just saying that to shut up Gabe and Jodi," Ben said as he leaned around Gabe to look at him.

"Why you gotta bring me into this?" Gabe said.

"Because you are the reason Alec is blowing it," JT answered. "If you could have just kept your mouth shut and dealt with the seat change, we'd all be at the table," he pointed over his shoulder, "enjoying a fun evening. But no, you had to go and be an ass."

Before Gabe could speak, Alec did. "This isn't Gabe's fault. Even if Penny was trying to shut him up at the table, on the way here, we talked about it, and she was being cagey even then." He signaled for another shot. "I guess my vacation fling is over."

"I can't believe I'm going to say this," JT said, "But you're blowing this out of proportion."

"Is he?" Ben asked, his voice quiet and calm. "I'm no expert, but from watching you guys together, other than when it comes to sex, it doesn't really seem like she wants to have anything to do with you."

Alec closed his eyes and thought back on the day and everything they'd done. While Annabelle and Ben had touched and kissed and made it very clear they were together, he and Penny hadn't done any of that. In fact, she almost avoided touching him or standing next to him.

He was an idiot.

This was nothing more than sex for her, and he'd gone and gotten feelings.

"I'm gonna head back to my room." He stepped away from the bar.

Gabe stopped him with a hand on his shoulder. "Don't

do that, man. Let's just enjoy our last night here. We can ditch the girls and do our own thing."

"Nah, you guys have fun. I'll be fine." He glanced over at the table, giving Penny one last look before he put her out of his mind forever. She had her head tilted back and her eyes closed. She looked beautiful.

But when did she not look beautiful?

With a sigh, he looked away and left her and everything they'd shared behind him.

Instead of heading to his room, he went to the beach, sitting down in the sand and watching the waves crash against the shore. He'd been so sure Penny was feeling the same things he'd been feeling. How had he been so wrong?

"I knew I'd find you here." Ben sat down next to him a while later. "You love the ocean."

He shrugged. "You should have stayed at dinner. This is your last night with Annabelle."

"Nah, we'll see each other when we get back."

"You guys have talked about it."

"Yeah, a little. She doesn't want a relationship, but she's willing to date." He sort of cringed. "But she's going to be dating other people too."

"Ouch, that had to sting." Just the thought of Penny dating other people made him jealous as hell. Even worse, he had no desire to date anyone else. He knew he'd only compare them to her.

"It does, but what am I supposed to do?"

"You could end it and walk away before you get your heart broken."

"I think you and I both know it's too late for that."

Silence settled around them, voices from the resort carrying out to the beach. Alec thought about Ben's words.

Ben was notorious for falling quickly, but for him, this was new. He'd never fallen this fast before. Hell, he'd never told a woman he loved her before. Not since high school when he knew it wasn't real love but wanted badly not to be a virgin anymore.

Since then, he'd never felt that all-consuming need to be with someone. He'd had girlfriends, but nothing so overwhelming that he missed them so badly when they weren't together.

It currently felt like there was a hole in his chest where Penny had ripped his heart out with her bare hands.

"I really thought she liked me," he confessed quietly.

"I know, man."

They sat together silently on the beach for another hour or so before walking back to their rooms. Once inside his room, he was bombarded with memories of Penny. The room smelled like sex, the covers were thrown on the floor and he saw a condom wrapper on the nightstand.

It was all overwhelming.

He sat down on his bed, dropping his head into his hands. He felt like such a fool for falling for Penny. What had he been thinking? She was on vacation and no one went on vacation looking for a relationship. If only he and his friends hadn't opted to stay an extra day. Then none of this would have happened.

He'd have met her, maybe had a night of sex and then gone home.

Sure the sex would have made him want more but their time together would have been cut short and nothing would have come from it.

He wished he could go back in time and change everything.

As soon as that thought popped into his head, he dismissed it. He didn't want to forget his time with Penny. It had been amazing and perfect and had made him happy.

He just wanted the pain to go away.

He doubted that would happen anytime soon.

Chapter Fourteen

Penny

"I'm going to his room and I'm going to kick the door down and break his dick." When Jodi got angry, she made threats that she in no way could keep.

Penny had just been told by JT and Gabe that Alec had left the restaurant.

He'd just left. Without talking to her or saying anything.

She wasn't as angry as Jodi. In fact she wasn't angry at all. She was sad. Sad that something she'd thought was so great turned out to be nothing.

Nothing at all.

"I think I'm going to skip dinner and go back to my room." She pushed back from the table. "I'll see you guys tomorrow."

As she walked away, Mya caught up with her. "Pen, hey." She grabbed her arm. "Are you okay? And be honest."

She shook her head. "Of course I'm not okay but he's made his decision. It's over. We're over."

"Do you want some company? We could watch movies and eat junk food like we did in college."

"I'd rather be alone. I promise you, I'm not going to do anything stupid. I'm just going to my room."

"Maybe you should do something stupid. You're too calm and it doesn't fit this situation. He left. Without saying anything. You guys have been having sex all day. That's not cool."

"So you want me to go knock on his door and ask what the fuck is going on?"

"Yes," she said definitively. "I thought you liked him and yet from the looks and sounds of it, you're just giving up and walking away."

"He walked away first!" she shouted into the night air. "How is that me giving up?"

"Because you're not fighting for what you want. Sometimes you have to fight."

She shook her head several times. "No, not in love. Love should come easy."

Mya crossed her arms over her chest and raised an eyebrow. "You calling it love tells me everything I need to know."

She threw her hands up. "I was just saying it as an example."

"I don't believe that's true but that's besides the point right now. Yes, love should come easy but you also have to work to keep the love. Sometimes people don't see what's right in front of their faces or they get scared."

"You think I'm scared?"

"Honestly? Yes. I think you're scared shitless because of how fast you fell for Alec and how fast he fell for you."

Penny turned away from Mya, needing to get away.

"You're wrong. I just want to be alone. Can't I just be alone?"

"If that's what you want, I'll leave you to it."

Penny walked away from her friend, trying not to think of what she'd said. She wasn't afraid. She'd jumped into whatever this was with Alec with both feet. She'd let it happen and wanted it to happen.

He was the one who was acting like a child by walking away.

Once in her room, she flopped down on the bed, staring at the ceiling. Turning her head to the side, she saw the chair they'd had sex on before dinner. Seeing it brought back all the memories of what they'd shared. Sadness overwhelmed her and before she knew it, she was hugging a pillow and crying herself to sleep.

Somehow she'd lucked out and not seen Alec at the resort before leaving for the airport. That was a good thing since her eyes were puffy and her face was splotchy and she was emotionally drained. If she'd had to see him, it would have been even worse.

"How are you doing?" Annabelle nudged her shoulder as they waited in the security line.

She shrugged, not really wanting to talk.

"I need to tell you something that I just found out, but I'm not sure how you're going to take it."

Penny looked at Annabelle. "What is it?"

"Ben told me that Alec took an earlier flight home."

Penny blinked, not sure she heard her friend right. "What do you mean?"

"Apparently there was a flight at seven this morning and Alec switched his flight to that one."

She was having a hard time wrapping her head around what Annabelle was saying. He'd taken another flight. All to avoid her.

Tears threatened to break through when she'd assumed she'd cried herself dry. She held them back as she closed her eyes and took a few deep breaths.

When she finally felt in control, she said, "That's probably good. Then I don't have to see him again."

The rest of the day, she kept to herself, not mingling or interacting with her friends or the guys. Even on the flight, Jodi knew better than to talk to her. All she wanted was to get home and crawl into her bed.

And forget that Alec Blair ever existed.

Which is exactly what she did. Sort of. For a week, she went about her life just like normal. Work, home, walks around the neighborhood, dinner alone and crappy sleep.

The crappy sleep she blamed on him. When she was awake, she could easily think of things beside him. When she was asleep, he was all she thought about. She remembered his kisses, the gentle ones and the fierce ones. She remembered the way he said her name when he came and how his face looked at peace after sex.

She remembered how she'd also felt so comfortable with a guy for possibly the first time ever.

Needing to stop her train of thought, she went to her kitchen in her small apartment and grabbed a bottle of wine from the fridge. It was Saturday night and she was home alone, about to drown her sorrows in alcohol.

Not a great message for an after school special. *Hey, kids, feeling depressed, why not drink?*

Yeah, she was no role model.

She twisted off the cap, because of course she drank cheap wine, and poured herself a very large glass. Both Mya and Jodi had invited her to do something but she'd turned them down, not ready yet to socialize beyond work.

Work had been hard enough.

As she drank, her thoughts kept going back to Alec. She was trying to forget him and yet it wasn't working. When she was just tipsy enough, she grabbed her phone and texted Annabelle.

Penny:
I need Alec's address.

Her phone immediately rang in her hand. She swiped across the picture of her and Annabelle in college that had popped up.

"Why are you calling me?" Her words weren't slurred but it was obvious she was drinking. Especially to someone who knew her as well as Annabelle did.

"Because you just asked me for Alec's address. I feel like that's the distress signal. Do I need to come over and save you from yourself?"

"I'm not in distress. I just need his address." She grabbed her wine glass, taking it with her as she paced around her small apartment.

"Why?"

"What do you mean why? I just want it."

Annabelle sighed. "Do you really think going over there

is a good idea? If you were sober, would you want his address?"

"First, I'm not drunk, I'm tipsy, and second, yes, I think I would want it." That was the complete truth. She'd wished for days that she knew where he lived.

"You're not going to drive, are you?"

"No, mom, I'll take an Uber." She rolled her eyes.

"Fine, let me text Ben and I'll get it."

Annabelle hung up and, in minutes, sent Penny a text with an address. Looking down at herself, she decided her sweats and baggy sweatshirt were just going to have to do. Pulling up the Uber app on her phone, she ordered a car and then grabbed her keys. She took one last drink of her wine and headed outside to wait.

When the car pulled up and she confirmed it was for her, she sat back, leaning her head against the seat, thinking of all the things she wanted to say to Alec.

The problem was, the things she wanted to do to him outweighed the things she wanted to say.

She was just starting to think this was a bad idea, when the car came to a stop and the driver announced they were there. It would be so easy to tell him to take her back home. To just forget this crazy idea and go back to forgetting he ever existed.

Except she couldn't.

Alec existed in a way that made her heart ache.

That settled it. She needed to do this for closure.

After she got out of the car, she stood on the sidewalk and watched the car drive away. This was it. She was going to confront Alec. Turning around, she didn't even really take in his house or surroundings as she walked up the sidewalk.

Before she could chicken out, she knocked loudly on the door.

It was only after she knocked that she saw there was a doorbell.

Oops.

She was just about to knock again when the door flew open.

"Penny," Alec said, confusion written all over his gorgeous face.

"Why'd you leave?" she blurted out loudly, letting her heart lead instead of her brain.

"Are you drunk?"

"No, I'm not drunk. I'll have you know I'm tipsy. There is a difference. And people who know me well know that difference. But you don't know me well so you wouldn't have a fucking clue, would you?"

"Why don't you come inside and we can talk and I can get you some water."

"I don't fucking want water." She stomped her foot like a child. "I want to know why you just left. The table, the restaurant and the resort." She held back from saying what she really wanted to say, which was why had he left her? That made her sound desperate and that was the last thing she needed.

"You were the one who was making this," he waved his hand between them, "into no big deal. Like it was just a vacation fling."

"That's bullshit," she spit out. "I initiated things."

"You initiated sex. That's it. What was I supposed to think?"

They were both practically yelling, but it felt good to get

it out. She'd let her emotions fester and now it was coming out as anger.

"What else was I supposed to initiate? Sex was our thing."

He shook his head, running a hand down his face. "That right there is why I left. All you wanted was sex."

Her mouth dropped open but words failed her.

That wasn't true. She'd wanted a lot more than sex. He was the one that only wanted sex.

"See you can't even deny it," he said. "Why'd you come here? To torture me some more?"

"I came here because I fucking miss you, you asshole!" Those words she didn't seem to have a problem saying when she probably should have kept them to herself.

"Well, I miss you too!" he yelled back.

They stood there, in the doorway to his house, staring at each other. He was so fucking good looking even in sweats and a hoodie. The gray sweatpants hung low on his hips, giving her just a glimpse of his skin.

Her fingers itched to touch him again.

She looked up into his eyes and saw they were filled with heat. She'd seen that look before. Several times.

"Penny," he whispered, barely audible.

That was all it took to break her.

She reached for him, locking her arms around his neck and pressing her lips against his. She felt his arms go around her back and heard him groan as they kissed.

It was explosive and full of passion, just like in Mexico.

Nothing had changed.

She felt them move and then vaguely heard the door slam shut before she was pushed up against it.

"Fuck, I've missed this mouth," he said against her lips as he continued to kiss her.

She was pulling at his clothes, trying to get him closer. She didn't want any space between them. If she could, she'd make it so she could feel him in her soul.

"Alec, I need you," she moaned as his hand slipped into her sweat pants, his fingers brushing against her already wet clit.

"I know what you need." He rubbed her clit a few times before he penetrated her with what felt like three fingers, with a force that had her stop breathing for just a second.

But there wasn't time to catch her breath because he didn't hesitate to start fucking her with his fingers. The pace was frantic as he kissed her and finger fucked her like his life depended on it.

She clung to him, not sure if she wanted to come quickly or hold off to make it last longer. She'd missed him so much that having it be over quickly seemed like a waste.

Her body, on the other hand, didn't care what her brain wanted. It wanted the orgasm that was barreling down on her and it wanted it immediately.

"Harder, oh god, harder," she begged against his lips.

"Come all over my hand. I want to feel it."

His words had her that much more desperate and when he hooked his fingers inside her, hitting that perfect spot, she detonated.

"Fuck yeah," he swore. The sounds were wetness were obscene as he continued to fuck her with his fingers. "Do it again."

"I can't, I can't." She wasn't sure that was true.

And that thought broke her out of her alcohol induced fog.

With his fingers still inside her, she dropped her head back against the door and said, "You didn't track me down." He didn't fight for her and that was what this was all about. If he'd wanted her for more than sex, he would have found her. She couldn't be the only one who gave a shit.

He stopped moving, and she shifted her eyes to see that he was looking at her oddly.

"I have to go," she pushed him away from her, immediately feeling the loss when his fingers left her body.

"Penny, stop," he said firmly.

"No, this was a mistake." She opened the door, running out and not looking back.

Looking back would only make it worse.

She needed to move on and forget all about Alec.

Chapter Fifteen

Alec

Everything inside him told him to run after her. Everything except the part where she'd looked right into his eyes and said it was a mistake.

"Fuck!" he swore, slamming his door closed.

He stared at the closed door, his brain and cock fighting him on what to do. His cock said go after her and his brain said it's not worth it.

Except it might be. She might be.

She'd accused him of not coming after her, and yet, it's all he'd wanted to do all week. He'd found out her address by doing a little online snooping and some luck when Ben had casually mentioned that Penny and Annabelle lived close to each other.

He'd driven past her place a dozen times, each time making the last-minute decision not to confront her.

He'd missed her like crazy and realized as soon as he'd

boarded his plane that he'd made a mistake. But, at the same time, she hadn't tried to contact him.

Until now.

Shit. He was a fucking idiot.

He pulled open the door and ran out toward the street, unaware of what he was doing. There was no way she was still out there. He turned right, which was the direction he saw her turn, and then came to a complete stop when he saw her frame in the dark, leaning against a light post.

"Penny," he said her name softly so as not to scare her.

"Go away, Alec."

He closed the distance between them until he was right in front of her. He touched her chin with his hand, lifting it until she looked him in the eyes. "I've driven by your apartment every day since Monday."

Her eyes opened wider, focusing on his. "What?"

"You said I didn't try to contact you, but that's not true. I found out where you lived, and every fucking day, I drove to your apartment. I just couldn't bring myself to actually go to the door and knock."

She shook her head. "That can't be true."

"Why would I lie?"

"I don't know, to get into my pants again."

He laughed until he realized she was being serious. "I think you and I both know that I don't need to lie to get into your pants."

He'd barely had time to take her in when he'd opened the door to his house and found her on his front step, but now he had the chance. She was in sweats, same as him except hers were pink. The sweatshirt she wore was ragged and old, telling him that she'd had it for some time.

It was also thin and he could very easily see that she

wasn't wearing a bra. Add in that, he knew from personal experience that she wasn't wearing underwear, and his dick was starting to want to join the party.

"Come back to my house and we can talk," he said, hoping like hell she'd take him up on his offer.

She shook her head. "If I'm alone with you, there won't be any talking involved."

Thinking quickly on his feet, he said, "Brunch tomorrow. There'll be lots of people around."

She bit her bottom lip, thinking. "I guess that could work." As she finished saying the words, a car pulled up. "This is me."

"Give me your phone," he said, holding out his hand.

"Why?" she asked, staring at her phone in her hand and then at him.

"Because I want your number and I don't have my phone with me."

She hesitated but then handed him her phone, which she'd already unlocked for him. He quickly typed in his number and sent himself a text so he would have hers.

"Tomorrow morning at eleven. Do you know where Eggsactly is?" It was a pretty well-known local breakfast place that he assumed she knew about.

She nodded.

He took that as a yes and stepped off the curb, opening the Uber door for her. "I'll see you then." He stepped back, letting her slip inside the car.

She gave him one last look, and it almost looked like she was having second thoughts about leaving. He knew he was having second thoughts about letting her go. But this is what she needed and he was going to try and do what she wanted.

"Get some sleep." He shut the door and then watched as the car pulled away.

He wasn't sure how long he stood there, but it was definitely long enough to no longer be able to see the car's tail lights before heading back to his house. After shutting the door and locking it, he searched for his phone. It was on the couch where he'd been sitting when Penny had knocked on his door.

And then knocked him on his ass.

For the second time in his life.

The fire she'd had when confronting him was just one of the things that made him like her—more than like her. But he couldn't go there yet. He had to earn her trust back, get her to like him again, and more, trust him.

He didn't want to play games, but just this once, he was going to have to keep some things close to his vest.

Like the fact that he was pretty sure she was it for him.

She'd run screaming like a kid in a haunted house on Halloween.

In the week since he'd seen her, he hadn't jerked off once. Well, that wasn't totally true. He'd tried once, but even with images of her in his head, he'd been unable to come. His body, and by body, he meant his dick, knew what it wanted. And it wanted Penny.

Tonight, though, his cock hadn't gone down since the moment he'd opened his door and saw her standing there. Even while they'd talked on the street, he'd been hard.

He was still hard.

Lifting his hand to his nose, he breathed in the scent of her that was still on his fingers. She'd come like a fountain, and he'd been seconds away from coming in his sweats.

Closing his eyes, he slipped his other hand down the

waistband of his sweatpants, gripping his cock. With her smell filling his memory, he stroked himself up and down. It wasn't long before he was on the verge of coming as he remembered how she'd begged so pretty for him against his front door.

A front door that he'd take with him if he ever moved.

His dick throbbed in his hand, but it wasn't until he once again put the fingers that had been inside her against his nose that his dick finally relented, coming over and over again on his hand and in his pants.

He dropped his head back, closing his eyes, waiting for the release to settle him. Only it never came. He wouldn't be satisfied until Penny was the one making him come.

What scared him the most was the thought that she'd never be his and for the rest of his life, he would never be satisfied again.

* * *

After a fitful night of sleep, he killed time with a workout and some frantic cleaning until it was time to leave to meet Penny. When he arrived, he was still twenty minutes early but was surprised to find her already there, sipping on what looked like a mimosa.

"Hey," he said when he approached the table.

"Hi," she said sort of shyly.

He took the seat across from her, trying to seem casual when he felt anything but. "I take it you made it home okay last night?" He'd wanted so badly to text her to make sure but opted against it so he didn't seem desperate.

"I did and then crashed hard." She shrugged. "That's what I get for drinking wine, I guess."

A waitress approached their table. "Sir, what can I get you to drink?"

"Coffee, please."

When she walked away, he nodded to Penny's drink and asked," Hair of the dog?"

She laughed. "Um, no. It's just orange juice but she brought it in this champagne glass. I'm not sure why."

They both laughed and for just a second, it felt comfortable again. Like it had in Mexico.

That feeling went away when she asked, "Should we talk about the elephant in the room?"

"I'm honestly not sure which elephant you're talking about. You showing up at my house, us doing what we did at my house, or me telling you I've basically been stalking you?"

She smiled, almost like she was going to laugh again, but stopped herself. "Let's start with you and work backward."

"You only want to do that so that you don't have to own up to missing me." He knew he was playing with fire, but teasing her was one of his favorite things. "But I'll play along." He paused to collect his thoughts. "I was an ass that last night in Mexico. When all the talk started about people switching seats so we could sit next to each other, I wanted you to want to sit next to me. I bailed when it started to seem like you didn't want that."

"I didn't say I didn't—" She shook her head. "No, I'm not going to interrupt. Keep going."

"I didn't want to leave. I wanted to spend that last night with you. When you didn't come knocking on my door, I got even more pissed and switched my flight to an earlier one." He shrugged. "I'm sorry for all that. When I got home, none of it mattered because I just missed you and wanted to see you. One day, Ben mentioned that you and Annabelle lived near each other, and from there, I could find out where you lived. I've driven by multiple times with the intent to knock, but never found the courage."

She let out a deep breath. "That's a lot to take in."

He watched as her hands fidgeted on the table. "It is, and I understand if you need time to process it."

She shook her head once but then stopped. "I don't know. What I do know is that my last night in Mexico was awful, and then when I got to the airport, even though I was dreading seeing you, finding out that you'd taken an earlier flight sucked." She sighed, shrugging slightly. "Maybe it's for the best. Maybe we should just leave this as what it was, a vacation fling."

"Is that what you want?" Please say no. He wasn't sure he could take it if she never wanted to see him again.

"I don't know."

"What do you know? Start there."

She looked up, her eyes meeting his. "I know I missed you, and I know I like the things we do together."

"I missed you too." He left out the last part because sex wasn't all he wanted from her. He wanted so much more.

The waitress interrupted them by dropping off their drinks. When she was gone, they sat silently for a few minutes before he spoke.

"What if we start over?" Even saying the words broke his heart. He didn't want to start over, but he'd do what he had to do if it meant winning Penny back.

"I'm not sure this is a bell we can unring." She gave him a quirky smile that melted his heart.

He laughed. "Yes and no. We can start over by just being friends. Nothing else."

She leaned in, whispering, "No sex?"

"No sex," he said. "We talk, maybe hang out, and see what happens." He shrugged as if it was no big deal when, in reality, it was the biggest deal. He had no clue how he was going to pull this off, but he'd do whatever it took to make her see they were meant to be together.

She leaned back in her chair, lifting her glass to her lips. She took a slow sip before setting it back down. "Okay, I'm game."

He felt the pressure and stress that he'd been holding onto for days leave his body at her words. "Great."

"So..." she drew out the word. "How do we start?"

"I think we've already started." He pointed to the table and their drinks. "Don't friends get brunch together?"

She laughed. "I guess you're right. Should we order some food because I gotta tell you, I'm starving."

"I imagine you are after all that alcohol last night."

She rolled her eyes. "I never should have opened that bottle of wine. It was a bad idea."

"I don't know. It led us to this moment, so it couldn't have been that bad of an idea."

"Blah," she said, sticking her tongue out. "Don't be sweet or cute. That needs to be one of the rules of this friendship."

"There are rules?" He raised an eyebrow in question.

"I think there have to be."

"If you say so." If it were up to him, there would be no rules. "So, rule number one, I can't be sweet or cute. That's pretty broad. How do I know if something constitutes sweet or cute?"

"You can't say sappy things, don't bring me gifts just because, and—" she pursed her lips. "Well, I can't think of anything else right now, but I'm sure I will."

"This goes both ways, you know. You can't be cute or

sweet either. So no adorable faces." He pointed at her.

"I don't make adorable faces."

"Ya do." He smirked.

"You can't do that!" she shouted. "No smirking."

"If I can't smirk, you can't wear sexy clothes like what you're wearing now."

She looked down at herself. "I'm literally in sweatpants and a hoodie."

"Like I said, no sexy clothes." Really, anything she wore would be sexy because it was her who he found sexy, not her clothing.

"Then the same goes for you. No gray sweatpants and no rolled sleeves."

He laughed. "Can I wear other colors of sweatpants? Or is it just gray that I can't wear?"

"Just gray," she said emphatically.

"Any other rules?"

"No touching. No hugs, or hand holding or even grazing of body parts. No touching period."

That one was going to be hard to follow because touching Penny was one of his favorite things. "I will do my best."

She bit her bottom lip. "Is this really going to work? Starting over? Being friends?"

"Why not?" He shrugged, trying to play it off as no big deal. "We'll just be two people who have seen each other naked hanging out. Lots of people do that." He was guessing. He had no clue and no desire to hang out with anyone else he'd had sex with.

Just Penny.

Because if his plan worked, they'd be more than friends.

She'd be his forever.

Chapter Sixteen

Penny

It was impossible to work when her mind was flooded with all things Alec.

From the way he looked, to the texts he sent her, to her nights alone in her bed, wishing it was him touching her instead of herself.

This friend thing was not going to work.

She didn't want to be friends with him. She wanted him to give her orgasms every day for the rest of her life.

No. No, no, no. She could not even put that thought in her head. She needed to keep this platonic. No sex, no orgasms. Just friendship.

It had been three days since their breakfast of truths, as she was calling it, and since then, she hadn't seen him, but they texted several times a day. Funny GIFs, silly stories, things like that. Nothing serious, or that could be considered sweet or flirty.

She missed the sweet and flirty.

Alec was good at the sweet and flirty.

When her phone dinged on her desk, she grabbed it quickly, hoping it was him. Instead, she saw a text from Mya.

Mya:
Lunch?
Penny:
Sure. Twenty minutes?
Mya:
Yup.

They didn't need to say more because when they met for lunch, they always went to the same place: Brickhouse. It was halfway between their offices and served the best burgers.

She finished what she was doing, grabbed her purse, and headed out. It was about a half-mile walk to Brickhouse, but she didn't mind it—especially on a day that was warmer, which it was.

Spring in Ohio was not always warm. The weather was erratic, and you never knew what to expect.

When she arrived at Brickhouse, she entered, and the hostess, Zoey, pointed to the back.

"She's already back there."

Penny thanked her and headed to their normal table in the back. They came here so often that they knew the staff and had their own table.

Maybe it was time to try something new.

"Hey," Mya said when she spotted Penny.

She slid into the booth. "How is it only Wednesday?" The week was dragging on, probably because she couldn't think of anything other than Alec.

"Right? Ever since we got back from Mexico, I can not get into a rhythm."

"I'm contemplating just moving there. I can work at a resort and serve drinks all day. Screw being in an office."

"I'm with you," Mya said. I can't believe I haven't seen you since we've been back. Is there anything new going on?"

She'd avoided her friends their first week home because she'd been in a funk, thanks to Alec. She was avoiding them now because she didn't know what was happening with him now that they were friends.

It was time to spill the beans.

"So, I'm sort of talking to Alec."

She waited for the shock, but it never came. Instead, Mya leaned back in her seat, smiling. "I was wondering how long it would take for the two of you to get your heads out of your asses."

Penny opened her mouth to speak but then closed it, needing a second to process.

"I can see I rendered you speechless. Come on, Pen, you and Alec had insane chemistry, and you live in the same damn town. There was no way you weren't going to see each other again."

"What if I told you that we've decided just to be friends?"

"I'd say you're idiots and make a bet on how long it takes one of you to break. My bet's on Alec breaking first."

"Well, at least you have some faith in me."

"Not really. I just think you're more stubborn."

"If I'm so stubborn, why did I break and show up at his house Saturday?" As soon as the words were out, she cringed.

"What?" Mya leaned over the table. "Tell me more."

Penny shook her head but decided she might as well just tell her friend everything. "I started drinking, and the more I drank, the more I missed him. I got his address from Annabelle and wasted no time in showing up there."

"What happened? What did he say?"

"I yelled at him for leaving the way he did, he yelled back a little and then we made out against his door."

"Made out, like just kissing or made out with more?"

Penny looked down at her lap. "More." She looked back at Mya. "But not sex."

"Then what happened?"

"I left, ran out, and said I couldn't do whatever it was we were doing. He followed and somehow got me to agree to breakfast the next morning, where we decided to be friends."

"Oh, he is good."

"What are you talking about?"

"He's making you think you're just friends to get you to fall for him. It's a classic for a reason."

"You read too much. Nobody does shit like that."

"Wrong. Everyone does shit like that. Look at Annabelle and Ben. He wants more but told her he's cool with their friends-with-benefits relationship and that he doesn't care if she dates other guys."

"How do you know he's not cool with it?"

"Because when she's not looking, he looks at her with puppy-dog eyes that would make even the most dog-hating person fall in love."

"You've seen them together since we've been home?"

"We went out Saturday. You know, when I invited you. Little did I know you had plans to get drunk and get it on with Alec."

"First, I was tipsy, not drunk, and second, we didn't get it on." She shrugged. "I mean, I got mine, but he was left, shall we say, unfulfilled."

"Man, I'm surprised he even wants to talk to you if you left him all hot and bothered."

Penny rolled her eyes.

"Hello, ladies," Clark, the owner, said as he approached their table. "Your usuals or something different?"

"Same for me," Mya said. Her usual was a burger and onion rings with a Dr. Pepper.

"Me too," she said, ordering her usual burger on a lettuce wrap with fries and water.

When Clark was gone, Penny turned back to Mya. "When you say you went out Saturday with Ben and Annabelle, does that mean the other guys were there?"

"Just Gabe. JT apparently had plans. But Jodi met up with us after the game."

Working for the local professional hockey team meant Jodi had to be at all home games and some away. She was pretty busy during the season.

"Is something happening with you and Gabe?"

"God no," Mya said. "He's a cool guy, but I don't know. I feel like I immediately friend-zoned him, and now I can't see him sexually at all." She fake vomited. "It would be like dating my brother."

"You don't have a brother."

It was Mya's turn to roll her eyes. "You know what I mean. But we do get along and have fun together."

An idea popped into her head. "We should all go out this weekend."

"You know I'm not stupid, right? You want to go out so that you can see Alec."

"I mean, I'd get to see you too." She knew she wasn't fooling Mya, but she had to try.

Mya laughed. "I'll willingly be your excuse if it means maybe you two will get to the finish line faster." She pulled out her phone. "I'll start a text chain and see who's in."

While Mya was typing away on her phone, Penny pulled out her own phone just to check it. Excitement bubbled up inside her when she saw she had a text from Alec.

Alec:
I was about to ask you what you were doing for dinner tonight but then I remembered we are just friends and I'm not allowed to be sweet. Is inviting you to dinner sweet?
Penny:
It is. You're going to need to rein that in.
Alec:
Is that a no to dinner?
Penny:
It's probably for the best.
Alec:
Well, I guess I'll just order takeout and eat all alone.

She smiled as her phone vibrated with another message. This one from Mya. She read over the message quickly. As she was reading, several texts came through.

"Looks like everyone is in," she said. She was waiting for Alec to answer but didn't have to wait long when his "sounds good to me" came through.

"I guess you're going to get to see your guy."

"Can we just not?" Penny said.

Mya laughed. "Whenever you're ready to admit to yourself that you want to be more than friends with him, I'm here to listen."

That wasn't going to happen. She needed to keep her wits about her when it came to Alec. She might wish he was the one giving her orgasms, but he'd already almost broken her heart once.

She couldn't take the chance of it happening again.

He was her friend, and it was going to stay that way.

Chapter Seventeen

Alec

This was a bad idea.

He was standing outside Penny's building, trying like hell to talk himself into going home.

Only his brain or heart or dick—whichever one was in charge—wasn't having it.

It was like his feet were glued to the ground.

He'd been at home, trying to think of anything or anyone other than Penny. And it worked for a few hours. But, when he laid down for bed, the moment his eyes closed, she was all he saw.

Which is how he'd ended up in his car driving to her apartment.

He had no clue what the plan was. Would he just drive by, or would he have the balls to actually knock on her door?

He was standing outside his car on the sidewalk, debating his options when he heard a door slam and feet running down the stairs. There was no time to move before the person came into view.

And he got the shock of his life.

"Alec." Penny came to a stop directly in front of him, her eyes wide in disbelief.

"Uh, hi." He didn't know what else to say.

"What are you doing here?"

"Would you believe me if I said I was in the neighborhood?" He was trying to be funny, hoping it wouldn't make him look like a complete stalker or, worse, pathetic.

She laughed. "No, I definitely wouldn't believe that."

It hit him that she was leaving her apartment on a Wednesday night at ten o'clock. That was odd. "Were you going somewhere?" Her outfit told him a lot. She was in sweatpants again, but this time, they were white and had what looked like paint stains on them. She had on an old, faded t-shirt with a jacket thrown over top of it. Her shoes were the most interesting thing. She was in flip-flops.

While the days had been somewhat warm recently, the current temperature was forty degrees. Her feet would be freezing in flip-flops.

There was no way she was going anywhere important.

He stayed planted where he was standing even though every part of him wanted to move closer to her.

"Umm, no, just came out for some," she cleared her throat, "air." She was looking down at the ground, kicking her foot around.

Then it hit him. She was coming to see him.

Holy shit.

This was kismet, if there ever was such a thing.

He took a few steps, moving toward her, stopping when

he was directly in front of her. He lifted her chin, forcing her to look at him.

"Where were you really going?"

Her eyes scanned his as she barely shook her head. "Nowhere."

"I don't think that's true." He wasn't sure how he knew she was coming to see him, but he did.

"Why are you here?" Her voice was quiet, barely audible.

"You know why I'm here." He dropped his forehead to hers, closing his eyes and relishing in the feel of touching her.

Fuck, he'd missed touching her. Even just this little bit was perfect.

"You're breaking the rules." Her words were choppy, almost like it was hard to breathe.

He opened his eyes, staring into hers. "Can we, just for tonight, pause the rules?"

"That's not a good idea." Her mouth might have said no, but her eyes were saying yes.

He reached out, grabbing her hip and pulling her against him. "Sometimes, what starts as a bad idea ends up being amazing."

She closed her eyes, her breathing picking up even more. There was a long beat of silence before she said, "Are you going to kiss me or not?"

Thank fucking god. "Not out here. Because if I kiss you, I won't be able to stop at just a kiss, and then we'd get arrested for indecent exposure or lewd sexual acts."

She smiled, biting down on her bottom lip. "I might be interested in some of these lewd sexual acts."

"Invite me inside." His voice was stern because his need for her was so strong.

She didn't hesitate to take his hand in hers and start walking back toward her building.

He followed her up the stairs and to her door, where she tried but failed to unlock the keypad with her code the first time. She tried again, this time the door unlocked with a loud click.

She turned to look at him before walking inside. "This is just a pause. It doesn't mean anything."

Those words punched him in the gut, but he didn't let it show. If she wanted to pretend this was nothing, he would let her. At least for now.

He nodded.

Penny opened the door and walked through with him right behind her. As soon as he shut and locked the door, he turned to face her. "Strip."

Her eyes heated. "Right here? You know I have a bedroom."

"We'll get there."

She cocked her head to the side. "If I have to strip, then so do you. And, I see you're also breaking another rule." She nodded her head to his pants.

His gray sweatpants.

"Yeah, well, I wasn't really thinking about what pants I was wearing when I left my house. And if we're talking about breaking the rules, you are breaking the one about being sexy."

She looked down at herself. "I'm dressed like a slob. You can't possibly think I'm sexy in this outfit."

"And yet, I do." He took a step closer to her. "But, I believe I gave you an order."

Her gaze held his as she replied, "And I gave you one too."

She was fucking perfect. Everything she said and everything she did. The ways she challenged him was such a turn-on.

"Together," he said, gripping the bottom of his hoodie, ready to pull it off.

She nodded and immediately kicked off her flip-flops.

He kept his eyes trained on her as they each undressed. When he pushed his sweat pants down his legs, and his cock sprang free, she sucked in an audible breath.

He looked down at his hard cock, then back up to her face. "It's not like you've never seen it before." He gripped his dick in his hand, stroking it up and down.

"I thought maybe I exaggerated how thick it was." She was fully naked now, every inch of her perfect body on display for him.

Except the hidden part between her legs.

His mouth was watering just thinking of her pussy.

Not willing to wait one more second before touching her, he grabbed her hand, pulling her against him. His mouth crashed down on hers in a kiss that was all fire and heat. Nothing about the kiss was slow or sweet.

This was the build up of passion they'd both been feeling since Mexico.

His fingers dug into her hips as they continued to kiss. Her own hands were in his hair, gripping and pulling it as she moaned into his mouth.

"Alec, don't make me wait," she said when he moved away from her lips and to her neck.

"Tell me what you want." He wasn't even sure how he was able to speak. He'd been dreaming of this moment since he'd walked away from her in Mexico, and now that it was here, talking was the last thing he wanted to do.

Except, he loved when she told him what she wanted and he knew she liked dirty talk. And, when it came to Penny and what she liked, he was willing to do whatever it took to make sure she had it.

Even if that meant using his big brain when his little brain was ready to take the lead.

"I need you to make me come," she moaned. "Please."

How could he ever deny a request like that? Especially when she begged so pretty.

He moved them back, lifting his mouth from her body only for a second to find the couch. When he was next to it, he pushed her down lightly while he immediately dropped to his knees on the floor.

Her legs spread on their own, and he got his first glimpse of her wet pussy. "Fuck," he swore. "I've missed this." He trailed a finger up her leg slowly until he reached her center. She was already so wet, and the moment he touched her, she moaned loudly.

"Goddamn, this pussy is begging for my mouth."

Her hips were gyrating and pushing forward, trying to find friction against something. He wasn't going to make her wait.

Without pause, he leaned in and licked right up her center.

"Oh god!"

He smiled with his mouth against her and then did it again just to hear her sounds. He loved them. After another lick, he decided to stop teasing her and himself and give them both what they wanted.

He flicked her clit over and over with his tongue before spearing her with it like he was fucking her. She was practically humping his face, something he didn't mind in the least.

"I'm gonna come," she said, her words breathless and broken.

That had been his goal, but he also wanted her to come so hard that just maybe she'd forget they were paused. So he pressed three fingers inside her as his tongue lapped at her clit. When he hooked them just the right way, she went off like a bomb, covering him in her release.

He didn't stop his movements, he couldn't. He loved being between her legs and loved it when she came so much that she drenched him. It was a new experience for him. One he wanted to have all the time.

Her body spasmed again, almost like she was having one long orgasm instead of individual ones. It was sexy as fuck, and he would lick her pussy for hours if this were the reward.

"You have to stop." She pulled on his shoulders. "I can't take it anymore."

He crawled up her body, kissing a path all the way to her mouth. "You can take that and much more." His lips touched hers and he let her taste herself on him before deepening the kiss.

His dick was hard and heavy between his legs, resting on her thigh as they kissed. He moaned into her mouth when he felt her hand on his cock, jacking him off slowly.

"I missed this dick," she murmured against his lips.

As much as he wanted to thrust inside her that instant, he also needed a condom and a bed. He stood, pulling her with him. "Please tell me you have condoms," he said as he looked around for her bedroom.

"Yes, in my room, which is over there." She pointed to the left, and sure enough, he spotted the door.

He looked back at her, taking in her flushed skin and sheen of sweat. He'd done that to her, and something about knowing that made him feel powerful. Bending his head, he kissed her quickly. Then he pulled her along to her room, with her laughing the whole way.

"In a hurry?" She let go of his hand, quickly flipping on the light before sitting down on the bed. She scooted back, making room for him to climb on.

"Yes." He kissed up her legs, alternating between the two.

"Condom," she moaned out as he continued to kiss up her body. He kissed each hip bone and her smooth belly.

"Where?" he asked, never taking his lips from her body.

"Drawer," she breathed out, pointing her arm to the side.

As much as he hated to stop touching and kissing her, he needed the condom for what he really wanted. Stepping off the bed, he opened the drawer, quickly scanning for what he was looking for. He found a pack of condoms and grabbed one, but his eyes lingered on what looked to be several sex toys.

"Is this your fun drawer?" He looked over at her and then back to the drawer.

She turned to her side, lifting up on her elbow and resting her head on her hand. "What if it is?"

The sexy smile she gave him practically stopped his heart. He had no clue how he was ever going to go back to being just friends after this. "Have you been using these?" He picked one up, looking at it. It was teal and shaped like a dick with a part that jutted out near the top that he assumed was for her clit.

"Maybe."

He dropped that one and picked one up that was small

and pink. This was just for her clit, and his heart was racing at the thought of her using it. "And this one, when was the last time you used it?"

He could see the blush on her cheeks. "Tonight."

He raised an eyebrow. "Tonight? Like tonight, tonight?"

She groaned, rolling to her back and covering her face with a pillow. "Yes," she said, her voice muffled by the pillow. She lowered it, looking at him. "That's why I was coming to see you. I couldn't get myself off, and I was frustrated."

He closed the drawer but didn't put away the toy. "Maybe you should try again." He held it out for her to take.

She took it from him but set it aside. "Later." She grabbed the condom from his other hand, quickly tearing it open. "I want the real thing first, and then we can play." She held out the open condom.

Her words had him almost swallowing his tongue. Later meant that she wanted more than this one time with him. He'd take that as a win.

At least for now.

Chapter Eighteen

Penny

What was she doing?

Sex with Alec was a bad idea. Never mind that he'd just made her come like a geyser on her couch. She was probably going to have to have the thing cleaned. Or throw it out. Because there was no way she didn't get it wet with her multiple orgasms.

She watched as he slid the condom down his length, and it was then she remembered why this was a good idea.

Because sex with him was better than any sex she'd ever had.

"Tell me what you want," he said, his voice gruff and demanding.

Her body shivered with need as she spread her legs and said, "Hard and fast."

It's what she'd been craving for days. Him inside her, fucking her hard while she forgot everything else, and for just a few moments, it felt as if they were the only two people in the world that mattered.

"I think I can make that happen." He kneeled on the bed between her legs, his dick inching closer to her pussy. He placed a hand beside her head as he leaned over her saying, "You might want to hold on to something."

Then, before she could even process his meaning, he plunged inside her in one hard thrust.

It was glorious.

"Fuck, I've missed this pussy." His guttural moan was music to her ears.

She'd wanted him to miss her as much as she'd missed him. Even though they were nothing more than friends.

Shit, she had to remember that.

Wanting him even closer, she wrapped her legs around his back and pulled his head down for a kiss. His kisses were addicting, and she wanted to be as closely connected with him as they made love.

Fucked. They were fucking.

It was not going to be easy to keep this platonic.

He'd yet to move inside her, and she whimpered against his lips, grinding her pelvis against him to try to get him going.

"Are you ready?" His words were low and almost devious against her mouth.

She knew what he was planning. He was going to fuck her into next month, and he was making sure she was good with that.

This man got her in so many ways. From knowing she wanted to be fucked hard to also knowing that asking made it even hotter.

As an answer, she held his gaze and dug her nails into his shoulders as she said, "Fuck me."

He groaned and then pulled all the way out of her body before thrusting back in. He did that slowly, twice, and then let go. She saw in his eyes the moment he did it. They turned black with hunger and need, and she imagined hers mirrored his.

He fucked her with abandon, their grunting and moaning and incoherent words filling the room. She scored his back with her nails, digging in and wishing he would never let go. She felt herself barreling toward release, but she wasn't ready.

If she came, it would be over, and then what?

As if he was reading her mind, he pressed his forehead against hers and said, "It's okay. You can let go. We are far from done tonight."

With that, she relinquished her thoughts to the night and let herself go. Her orgasm came on fast and hard, with her gasping for breath. Alec closed his eyes, grunting loudly as he slammed into her faster and faster until he threw his head back, her name a whisper on his lips as he came.

A feeling of contentment came over her, and she closed her eyes to try to preserve it. She wanted to remember this feeling on days when she felt lost and alone.

The part of her brain that was a traitor said, *"You wouldn't be alone if you were with Alec."*

She immediately shut that thought out. Yes, she liked him, and yes, he was amazing at sex, but she wasn't ready to risk her heart.

That answer was a resounding no.

"Holy hell," he said as he rolled off her. She watched

through sleepy eyes as he dealt with the condom, flipped off the light, and then returned to bed.

When he pulled the comforter up over them and wrapped his arm around her neck so she'd have to lay her head on his chest, she looked at him, his face very visible in the dark. "I thought we weren't finished?"

"We aren't, but I thought we could take a little catnap to regain our strength."

"What about the rules? I don't think you're supposed to stay the night." Even as she said words, she rested her head on his chest and snuggled deeper into his side.

"In case you forgot, we're on a pause, and even if we weren't, I don't remember a no sleepover rule."

She giggled. "I think it was implied in the no touching rule." A rule she was currently breaking many times over.

His hand touched her head and started stroking her hair. "Paused, remember? I can touch you all I want."

"Do you think we're being smart, pausing like this?" She toyed with the hair on his chest mindlessly.

"I think the cat's out of the bag at this point." His voice sounded sleepy.

Like him, she was tired. She hadn't had a good night's sleep since Mexico, and if Alec was going to be in her bed all night, she should probably take advantage and get some sleep.

Rules be damned.

* * *

As she woke up, she realized two things immediately. She was plastered against Alec like he was a life preserver on a sinking ship, and that she'd just had the best night's sleep in almost two weeks.

This was not good.

Hoping he was still asleep, she extricated herself from his body and slowly got out of the bed. It was still dark outside, so she wasn't quite sure of the time but when she looked down at him, her heart jumped just a little even though she told it to stop. He looked peaceful in sleep. His usually clean-shaven face had a hint of stubble and his hair was a mess both from sleep and her fingers that she'd tangled in it when he was between her legs.

She gave him one last glance before grabbing a shirt off the ground and getting out of there. If she stayed any longer, she was afraid she'd crawl back into bed with him and never leave.

In her small kitchen, she saw that it was only five-thirty. Way too early to be up, considering the energy she'd used the night before, and way too early for work. But there was no way she was going back to bed with Alec in there.

It was time to unpause and go back to their rules.

She was sitting on the couch, sipping coffee, when she heard Alec walking into the room. She looked up just as he stepped into her view.

He was completely naked.

"What the hell! Put some clothes on." She shielded her eyes as if she hadn't already seen all of him multiple times.

It was mainly because she was afraid that if she kept looking at his naked body, she'd do something stupid like fall to her knees and put his dick in her mouth.

"I would have, but all my clothes are out here." He pointed to the pile of clothes that she'd folded neatly on her coffee table before she'd sat down.

"You could have at least covered yourself." She grabbed the pile, handing it to him.

He smirked. "Are you worried you'll see something you might like?"

"Shut up." She shoved his shoulder. "Go get dressed. I need to start getting ready for work."

He placed the clothing in front of his dick, giving her a little bit of a refrain from his body. "I need to get home so I can get ready for work too." He moved around to the back of the couch, and she heard ruffling, assuming he was getting dressed.

Less than a minute later, he stepped back into her view, fully clothed. "So..." He scratched the back of his head.

"Pause is over," she said, trying to sound stern. "I mean, last night was fun, but we need to stick to the original rules."

"Fun," he said in a huff, shaking his head. "Yeah, okay. Pause is back on." He walked in front of her, heading to the door. He looked back over his shoulder, his eyes meeting hers one last time before he pulled the door open and walked through it.

When it closed behind him, she sank back into her couch, closing her eyes and wondering what the fuck she was doing.

Their night together had been outstanding. Not only that, but she was coming to know him through the texts and the time they'd spent together in Mexico. She liked who he was. And she really liked that he'd showed up at her apartment on a Wednesday night at ten o'clock because he couldn't stay away, even though she'd made him agree to her stupid rules.

For the first time in her life, a guy was putting himself

out there and what was she doing? Keeping him at arm's length.

She was a fool, but a fool whose heart would still be whole when it was all said and done. Was that worth not trying, though? She didn't know and wasn't sure where to look for the answer.

She was a twenty-five-year-old woman who had never really been in love and had no clue how to determine if what she was feeling was love or just infatuation with fantastic sex.

Was anyone an expert in that area? Because she'd pay big money to have someone tell her what to do.

Glancing at the clock, she saw it was late enough to text her friends.

Penny:
I did something stupid last night.
Jodi:
I'm guessing the "something stupid' was actually "a someone"?
Mya:
Please tell me you didn't sleep with Nick.
Annabelle:
You slept with Nick? You hate him.
Penny:
The someone wasn't Nick. It was Alec.
Mya:
He finally wore you down, I see. That didn't take long.
Jodi:
What are you talking about, Mya? I thought Penny and Alec weren't in contact since we got back.
Penny:

It's a long story, but we have been talking. Just this week.
Annabelle:
I think that's great.

Her phone vibrated in her hand, and she saw that Jodi was initiating a FaceTime with all of them.

She answered, knowing full well that Jodi wanted all the details.

"What the hell, Pen. You've been talking to Alec and didn't tell me?"

"Leave her alone," Annabelle said before Penny could speak.

"It just happened on Saturday, and I haven't fully processed what's happening yet."

"You've been sleeping with him since Saturday?!?" Jodi's voice shouted over the phone.

"Calm the fuck down," Mya said. "She hasn't been sleeping with him since Saturday. Although, if you want to get technical..."

"Mya, you aren't helping," Penny said. I'll tell you everything if you all would just chill for a minute." She went on to tell them the whole story, starting with her showing up at his place last Saturday and ending with him walking out the door that morning.

"He doesn't want to be friends with you," Annabelle said when her story ended. "Or just friends, I should say."

"I agree with her," Jodi said. "Not only that, but I think I'm starting to like him for you."

Jodi was the one person she could count on to be reasonable, and now she was on board. "What do you mean?"

"He's not giving up. He's making sure you know that he's

going to be there. Always. A guy who does that is a guy worth keeping."

"So what, you're saying I should just give in?"

"Why are you hesitant?" Mya asked.

Her mind and heart decided that was the moment when they'd collide. "BECAUSE HE ALREADY LEFT ME ONCE!" As soon as the words were out, she realized that's what was holding her back.

"Oh, Pen," Annabelle said. "I know that hurt, but I don't think you can judge him based on what happened in Mexico. It all happened so fast, and you guys barely knew each other."

"She's right," Mya said.

"But..." She swallowed the tears that were threatening to come out. "What if he leaves again?"

"Let me ask you this," Jodi said. "Would your heart be any less broken in a few weeks or a few months? Broken is broken."

She shrugged, thankful for FaceTime so her friends could see her, and she didn't need to speak.

"You don't have to make a decision today," Mya said. There is no pressure or timeline here. Just think about it."

"And in the meantime, maybe have great sex," Annabelle said, breaking the mood.

They all laughed and chatted for a few more minutes about other things before getting off the call. She felt better after talking to her friends, but she still had no clue what she should do.

The fear of a broken heart for the rest of her life was real. Alec was different from any other guy she'd ever met, and she was positive that getting over him would not be quick or easy if she could even do it.

The problem was she was afraid she was already in too deep. Even if they stayed just friends, she was sure she'd compare every other guy to him which would, in turn, mean she'd be single and alone the rest of her life.

Jodi might be right. A broken heart was a broken heart whether it happened now or later.

Chapter Nineteen

Alec

You'd think that sex with the woman he loved—and yes, he finally realized it was full-fledged love—and then finally getting a good night's rest would have put him in a good mood.

That was not the case.

All because he let her words get to him right before he'd left.

He'd been prepared for her to distance herself from him after their night together. He was starting to understand her and how she worked and knew she'd be ready to go back to their rules. But even being prepared hadn't stopped him from the emotional overload of feeling like he was nothing more than a night of sex for her.

"Yo." He looked up from his computer and saw JT standing there. "Wanna grab coffee?"

Alec checked the time and saw he had plenty of time

before his first meeting. "Sure." He shut his laptop, pushing back in his chair.

"You were here early this morning," JT said as they walked toward the elevator. "And you look like hell."

After he left Penny's, he went home, showered, dressed, and went straight to work. He thought it would be a good distraction.

He'd been wrong.

"I'm sorry not all of us can be as fancy as you." JT was known for always being dressed immaculately. No wrinkles, no hair out of place. It was a joke that even the soles of his shoes were probably clean.

"Grouchy too," JT said. "If I didn't know any better I'd say you were having woman troubles, but since you are still hung up on Penny, I know that can't be true." The elevator opened and they got on. "Wait a minute, is this about Penny?"

He might as well spill the beans. Come Saturday when they were all together, it would most likely come out. "We've been talking."

"Whoa, that's a twist I did not see coming." He rolled his eyes, showing his sarcasm. "It was pretty obvious that there was no way Mexico was the end of whatever it was you guys had going on."

"She showed up at my place Saturday and since then, we've decided to be friends." The doors opened and they stepped off the elevator. "We even have rules." He shook his head that he'd been stupid enough to agree to any of those dumb fucking rules.

"These I need to hear," JT said.

They walked out of the building, turning right on the sidewalk towards a local coffee shop they liked to go to.

"There's a no-touch rule, and I'm not allowed to be sweet or cute or wear gray sweatpants." He lifted his arms. "Oh, and I can't have rolled sleeves in her presence."

JT was laughing. "Gray sweatpants? That's very specific."

"I said the same thing." He couldn't help but laugh too.

"Did you give her rules?"

"I told her she couldn't be sexy or flirty. Which is ridiculous because everything she does is sexy."

"I take it your bad mood is because these rules are getting to you?"

He cringed. "It's more because last night, we broke all the rules."

"Oh boy! Now we're getting somewhere." JT opened the door to the coffee shop. "Tell me everything."

"You're going to have to get your sexual kicks somewhere else." The things he did with Penny were just for him.

"I don't want the sexual details. I want to know how it came to be that you broke all the rules."

He sighed as they stepped up to the counter. He quickly ordered a vanilla latte, paid, and then moved to the side so JT could order. When JT finished and moved to stand beside him, Alec filled him in on what happened.

"I couldn't stay away last night and drove to her apartment. As I was standing outside, looking at her building, she came rushing out like she was in a hurry to get somewhere. Only she wasn't dressed like she wanted to be seen in public."

"Oh, please, tell me she was coming to see you."

Alec pointed at him. "You'd be correct."

"This is like the perfect rom-com movie."

"Since when do you watch rom-coms?"

167

"Hey, I have layers. Now, what happened next?"

"After some back and forth, we decided to pause our rules for the night." Just saying the words had him remembering the way she'd looked when she'd asked him to kiss her.

"Let me guess. Now you're sad and grouchy because the rules are back on."

He nodded. "That about covers it."

"Even though you knew she'd go back to the rules?"

He nodded again. "I know, I'm an idiot."

"You're not an idiot, you're just a guy in love with a woman who is lying to herself about being in love with you."

"She's not in love with me." If she was, why was she pushing him away?

"Yeah, she is." JT raised his eyebrows. "You're just blind to it."

The barista called their names and they both stepped forward to grab their coffees. Once outside, he looked at JT. "How can you be so sure?"

"I mean, I guess I don't know for sure, but I've seen you guys together and the way she looks at you. It's more than friendship and more than just fucking. She likes you and wants to be with you."

He took a drink of his coffee. "I'll see her again on Saturday when we all go out. What do you think I should do?"

He shrugged. "Hell if I know. I'm no expert on relationships."

"Now you have no advice for me when just moments ago, you were full of it."

"I told you...layers."

"I fucking hate you."

The conversation changed to work as they walked back

to the office and when they got up to their floor, they ran into Gabe as they were coming off the elevator.

"Just who I was looking for," Gabe said.

"Me or him?" Alec pointed at himself first and then at JT.

"You. Mya mentioned that you and Penny have been, shall we say, talking. I thought I'd see what's going on."

"Wait," JT, stepped in front of Alec and put a hand on Gabe's shoulder. "You've been talking to Mya?"

"Yeah," Gabe said as if it was no big deal. "We're friends."

Alec couldn't be sure, but the tick in JT's jaw told him that this wasn't something he wanted to hear.

Could JT like Mya? That was an interesting turn of events. One he could use to his advantage with Penny.

"Can it wait?" Alec asked Gabe. "Say lunch? I really need to get to this meeting." He still had fifteen minutes before the meeting started but he wanted that time to text Penny.

"Yeah, just come get me when you're ready."

Alec barely said goodbye before walking away and returning to his desk. Once there, he pulled out his phone and texted Penny.

Alec:

Has Mya mentioned Gabe at all?

Penny:

She says they're friends. And she literally almost gagged when I suggested they might be more. Why?

Alec:

Gabe mentioned her just now and I swear JT looked like he was going to punch him.

Penny:
Wait. What? Are you saying you think JT likes Mya?
Alec:
That's what I'm saying.
Penny:
Holy fucking shit. I don't know what to do with this info.
Alec:
*We might be able to tell more when we're all together on
Saturday.*
Penny:
*Oh that's smart. We can watch them and see how they act
around each other.*
Alec:
This could be interesting.
Penny:
I can't wait for Saturday. See you then!

He continued to stare at his phone long after they'd stopped texting. It was as if he thought staring at it would somehow make her appear. When his computer dinged, alerting him of his meeting, he set his phone aside and jumped up, heading for the conference room.

He saw Ben already in there and took the seat next to him. "Morning."

"Hey," Ben said.

The meeting started, but Alec's mind was occupied with all things Penny. He knew she liked him and wanted to be more than just friends, but something was holding her back.

Had she been hurt before? Has some guy broken her heart and made her gun-shy about getting into a relationship? Or was it really just that he'd fucked up in Mexico?

There was a noise and when he looked up, he saw that everyone but Ben had left the room.

"It's a good thing I knew what the fuck we're doing on this project," Ben said. "Because you were not paying any attention."

"Shit," he said, running his hands down his face. "Did I miss anything?"

"Nah," Ben said laughing. "It was the normal shit and nobody even noticed that you weren't paying attention."

Relief swept over him. "That's good."

"You okay?"

"Yeah, I just have a lot on my mind." They both stood up and walked together out of the conference room.

"I assume the thing on your mind is Penny?"

"You'd be right." He needed a break from all things Penny. "How are things with Annabelle?"

"Nothing new. She wants to date other people and I'm just the sucker who has to sit around and let it happen." Ben looked defeated and Alec wished there was something he could say to help his friend feel better.

But he had his own woman who refused to commit. If he had advice, he'd use it himself.

"I'm sorry, man."

Ben shrugged. "At least I get to have her in my life."

They parted ways, each of them going back to their own desks. When he sat down, he saw he had a few missed texts on his phone.

His heart sped up when he saw they were from Penny.

Penny:
I don't regret last night.
Penny:

I'm just not sure we can do it again.

He let out a breath, leaning back in his chair.

It might not seem like it, but he was starting to understand Penny pretty well, and for her to send a text like that meant she had feelings for him—more than just friendship feelings.

Which, of course, he'd assumed but he'd also been somewhat unsure about.

A conundrum if ever there was one.

What this meant for him was that on Saturday when he saw her, he needed to bring his A game. She needed to see what things could be like if they were together.

How he was going to show her, he had no clue.

Chapter Twenty

Penny

This was impossible.

How was she supposed to pick an outfit when one of their rules was nothing sexy?

Something Alec had reminded her of when he'd texted her that morning. He'd listed things he found sexy, which was almost everything.

Tight jeans, loose jeans, dresses, tops that showed any skin at all, tops that were baggy, sweats, leggings, t-shirts.

The man was a lunatic if he thought she looked good in all those things.

She'd tried to tell him that wasn't possible when they were going out in public and he asked if that meant she wanted to pause again.

She'd emphatically told him no, not unless he'd let her just pause that one rule. Of course, he'd refused, and now she was lying on her bed, surrounded by every piece of clothing she owned, completely clueless about what to wear that wasn't considered sexy.

Grabbing her phone, she dialed Annabelle and put the phone on speaker.

"Hey," Annabelle said, sounding way too chipper.

"Help," was all she said.

"I'm going to need a little more info."

"I have nothing to wear. One of the rules with Alec is that I can't dress sexy."

"That's easy, wear jeans and a plain top."

If only it were that easy. "Unfortunately, Alec has a long list of things he considers sexy and that's basically everything."

Annabelle laughed. "Can't you just ignore the rule?"

"Not if I don't want to unpause."

"I'm too sober for this conversation," Annabelle said. "What happens if you unpause again?"

"All the rules go out the window and he's allowed to touch me and kiss me and do all the other things I want him to do." She sat up, staring at the clothing strewn around her room.

"I'm not sure I see the problem. You want him to touch you, so wear something sexy and unpause."

She made it sound so simple.

"We're friends."

"Naked friends."

"Ugh!" she screamed into the empty room.

"Pen." Annabelle's voice was calm. "I've known you since freshman year of college when you walked into my dorm room and basically told me we were going to be friends. Where is that girl? She was strong and confident and didn't take no for an answer."

"I think I left her in Mexico that last night when he walked away from the table." She hated the unsure person she'd become since then and it was all Alec's fault. If he'd just stayed and talked to her maybe she'd still be that person.

"I think you need to find a way to get her back because if she could see this version of you, she'd be appalled."

"Fuck it," she stood up, grabbing her favorite jeans.

Her favorite tight jeans.

"I'm wearing what I want, Alec be damned."

"There she is." She heard Annabelle clap over the phone. "Is the crisis averted because I too have to get ready and I plan on looking super sexy to pick up a hot guy."

"Are you talking about Ben?"

"No, why would I pick Ben up? I'm already sleeping with him."

"Are you really going to pick up another guy with him there?" She wasn't judging, but she did feel bad for Ben.

"He knows we're just friends. He dates and sleeps with other people, too."

Penny didn't believe that for one second. Plus, from what she knew, they were together a lot. When did either of them have time to sleep with someone else?

"Well, then I wish you luck finding a hot guy to hook up with."

They hung up and Penny took her newly founded confidence and dressed in an outfit that made her feel sexy and happy. Screw Alec and his damn rule.

When she looked in the mirror at herself, she saw the woman she'd always been but had lost for a little while. She still wasn't sure what she was going to do about Alec and how she felt about him, but that was just going to have to wait.

Tonight, she was going to have fun.

* * *

The bar they'd picked to meet at was one she'd been to many times. It was busy, but not so crowded that you had to wait twenty minutes to get a drink from the bar. When she arrived, she found Gabe already there, sitting at the bar, sipping on something.

"Hey," she said as she walked up next to him. "I see you're an early bird like me."

"It's my best and worst quality."

She laughed. "Same. My mom says I don't know how to be late." She signaled for the bartender and ordered a tequila and soda.

"The struggle is real," he said with a smile.

"Fire that asshole from Mexico yet?"

He laughed. "Not fired but he's about to hate his job."

"Ohh, what did you do?"

"I moved him to another team and his boss just so happens to be a woman."

She threw her head back laughing. "Oh my God, that is even better."

"What's so funny?" Ben joined them.

"I was just telling Penny how I moved Matt to Sandi's team."

"Oh yeah, he's seriously going to hate that. I bet he quits before the month is out."

"We can only hope," Gabe said, saluting Penny with his drink.

"I see you said 'fuck the rules'," Penny heard Mya's voice before she actually saw her.

"Mya," Penny said her name in warning. She had no clue if Alec told his friends what was going on with them.

"What rules?" Gabe asked because, of course, he would. He was a curious guy.

"Oh, little miss rule breaker here isn't supposed to dress sexy per the rules she has with Alec." Mya grabbed Penny's drink from her hand, taking a sip. "Ugh, soda water. I hate soda water."

Penny stole the drink back. "That's what you get for stealing my drink and blabbing my personal business."

"Hold up," Ben stepped between them, "You and Alec have rules?"

Penny sighed, looking at Mya. "I hate you." She looked at Ben and Gabe. "We have decided to be friends and along with that friendship comes some rules to keep us from straying into...shall we say non-friendship activities." However, that hadn't worked well for them so far.

Gabe laughed. "We're all adults. You can say sex."

"I want to hear all these rules," Ben said.

Before she could answer, a voice that she knew all too well was right behind her. "Go ahead, Penny. Tell them the rules. Although it seems like we've thrown them out the window."

She shivered just hearing his deep voice. "Oh, hey, Alec." She turned around to get her first look at him and realized that was a mistake.

He looked fucking sexy as hell. And yet, he'd followed the rules. He was wearing a button-down shirt with jeans, but the sleeves were down and not rolled up.

She was pretty sure she'd lost the ability to speak with how sexy he was. Thankfully, Mya spoke up.

"She's not allowed to be sexy, and unless it's opposite day, she failed."

Alec raised an eyebrow, silently asking her to explain.

How she knew that she had no clue. But somehow she understood this man.

"I, uh, attempted to dress for the rules but after trying on everything in my closet, decided I wanted to wear something that made me feel sexy, rules be damned. And honestly, how am I supposed to know what you find sexy?" She pressed a finger to Alec's chest. "I was in the ugliest thing the other night, and that didn't seem to matter."

"What happened the other night?" Gabe asked, looking between them.

She saw Mya slap Gabe's chest. "Shhhh."

Alec looked down to where her finger was touching his chest. "If we are ignoring the rules..." he crossed his right arm over his lower body under her where her arm was. When she looked down, she saw he had begun rolling the sleeve on his left arm. "I guess I can do this."

She immediately pulled her finger from his chest as if it was burning her. And it sort of was. She was on fire from the inside at the heat he was putting off. "Now you're just being ridiculous."

He continued to roll his sleeves ever so slowly like he was toying with her. "So the rules only apply to me and not you?"

"I feel like a voyeur," Ben said loud enough for them to hear, even though he was obviously whispering.

"You and me both," Mya said.

Alec tilted his head to the side in question. "What's it going to be? Rules for both of us or no rules at all."

She groaned in frustration, but then remembered the strong, confident woman who'd made the decision to defy the rules in the first place. That Penny could handle a little flirting and touching with a guy. Even if it was a guy who made her heart beat a hundred times faster than usual and knew just how to ease the ache between her legs.

The rolled sleeves might be a problem because forearms were a weakness of hers and Alec had terrific forearms.

She could hold strong, though.

Probably.

"I guess we can drop the rules." Saying those words was almost freeing.

"I'm not sure this has the effect you think it does," Mya said. "It's not as if you guys were adhering to the rules anyway." She laughed, entwining her arm through Penny's.

"Enough about us," Penny said. "Should we grab a table?"

"I have a hightop reserved," Gabe said, pointing to a table right behind them.

"Why does that not shock me," Mya said, laughing.

Just as they moved to the table, Annabelle arrived, going straight to Ben. "Hey, guys."

Penny pulled out a stool to sit down and Alec just so happened to sit down in the one next to her. As everyone chatted, he leaned in closer to her. "You look sexy as fuck."

His whispered words had her clenching her legs together. It reminded her too much of when they were in bed, and he was whispering all the dirty words she liked so much.

"You look pretty hot yourself." She turned her head, looking him up and down.

He laughed. "We should have known the other night that these rules weren't going to last long."

"Just because we don't have rules doesn't mean I'm going

to sleep with you again." There she'd said it. Even if she didn't believe it.

"I guess I'll just have to try and change your mind." His hand landed on her thigh, and she sucked in a breath at just that tiny touch.

Yeah, she was screwed.

Chapter Twenty-One

Alec

Penny breaking the rules was not shocking.

Penny saying they were dropping the rules was.

She'd been so adamant that they have rules, and even when they'd paused them the other night, she'd been sure to put them back in place the next morning.

He wasn't complaining, though. He hated the rules. He wanted her to dress sexy and flirt with him. And he absolutely wanted her to touch him whenever she wanted.

Without the rules, it also meant he could touch her, something he was looking forward to doing anytime he felt like it.

In fact, his hand was on her leg at that very moment, and he was enjoying the hell out of the way he could see she was panicking internally.

Oh, on the outside, she was calm and cool, but he knew her and knew that having his hand on her leg was driving her crazy.

In a good way.

She might try to deny it, but she wanted him just as much as he wanted her. Whether or not that want transferred to love was another thing entirely.

He'd just have to do his best to make it happen.

"Has anyone heard from Jodi?" Annabelle asked.

"She's coming, but had to stop by work first," Mya said with an eye roll. "I swear that team would crumble if she wasn't there."

"What about JT?" Ben asked.

"I'm right here, asshole," JT came up behind, startling them all. "What did I miss?"

"Oh, nothing much," Gabe said. "Just Penny and Alec ditching some silly rules they'd made for when they saw each other."

"You dropped the rules?" JT raised an eyebrow at him.

Alec pointed to Penny. "Penny did it when she tried to kill me with a heart attack, showing up here looking like this."

"Oh my god!" Penny exclaimed. "I'm dressed normal. You'd think I was wearing a dress with barely any of me covered."

"Do you have a dress like that?" Alec asked. "Because I wouldn't be opposed to seeing you in something like that." Honestly, she could wear a paper bag and he'd get turned on.

She leaned into him, nudging his shoulder with hers. "Is sex all you think about?"

"Uh, duh," JT said. "We're guys."

"You'll be shocked to hear that girls also think about sex a lot," Annabelle said.

"She's right," Mya said. "In fact, I'm thinking about it now with that guy over there."

"What guy?" JT said, his tone demanding with a hint of annoyance.

Mya smirked. "Wouldn't you like to know?" She walked away, and Alec watched his friend watch her make her way across the bar.

"Damn," Penny whispered so only he could hear. "I think you're right."

"I told you," he also whispered. "Something is up with him."

"I need a drink," JT said in apparent frustration.

"Me too," Alec quickly said. He hated to leave Penny's side, but this was his chance to get some info on his friend.

At the bar, they both ordered, and then Alec asked, "What's up with you and Mya?"

JT looked shocked by the question, immediately shaking his head. "Nothing."

"There may be nothing right now, but I think you'd like it to be something."

He frowned. "She just irritates me, and I feel like she does it on purpose. Like why did she need to go talk to that guy? Aren't we all here together?"

"She's allowed to talk to people...guys, if that's what she wants. Especially if you haven't made your interest known."

He shook his head. "I'm not interested."

"Could have fooled me." He took the beer the bartender handed him, handing the guy a card to start a tab.

"I'm not sure you should be giving me dating advice."

He wasn't wrong. There were times he felt he had a handle on his feelings for Penny, and then times he felt so out of control that he did stupid things like show up at her apartment and suggest rules.

"You might be right." They took their drinks and headed

back to the table. His steps faltered when he saw the seat he'd been sitting in, the one next to Penny, was occupied.

By a man.

A man who had Penny laughing.

A man who was built like he spent all his time in the gym. His muscles were literally bulging through his shirt.

His insides turned to fire, and not in a good way like when he had Penny under him. This was rage, pure and simple. When he reached the table, he slid into the space between Penny's stool and Annabelle's, who was on the other side of her. He would have preferred to separate Penny from the guy who was obviously hitting on her, but he was trying not to come off as a jealous asshole.

He knew Penny well enough to know that would not go over well.

"Hey," he said to get their attention.

Penny turned her head to look at him, biting her bottom lip as she did so. "Um, Alec, this is my co-worker Damian. Damian, this is Alec."

"Nice to meet you," Damian said. "I saw Penny over here and had to come say hi."

"I bet you did," he said under his breath, which had Penny elbowing him in the side. "So you guys work together. That's cool." Being nice was going to make him vomit.

"We don't technically work in the same department," Damian said. "But we've had to connect when there are issues."

"Damian is in legal," Penny said.

Fucking great. He was a lawyer. How was he supposed to compete with that? Luckily, he was saved from a snide comment by Jodi, who picked that perfect moment to arrive.

"Let the party start!" She announced, and somehow she already had a drink in her hand.

"The party already started," Annabelle said.

"I can see you're busy," Damian said. "I guess I'll see you at work."

"You can stay," Penny said sweetly.

"Nah, I'll let you have your fun." He stepped away from the table.

"See ya, Damian!" Alec shouted and even he could hear the edge in his voice. He leaned into Penny, his lips right on her ear. "Is that the kind of guy you like? Muscles and money."

She turned her head so quickly, looking at him in confusion. "What are you talking about?"

"Damian," he said, disgust in his voice at speaking his name. "It's obvious he likes you."

Her head was shaking before he even finished his words. "We just work together. He's a nice guy."

"He wants you." Even saying the words made him angry.

She raised an eyebrow. "Are you jealous?"

"Sounds like that to me," Jodi said before Alec could answer for himself. "Jealousy is a red flag. A big red flag." She pointed her drink at Alec.

"I'm not jealous." He was so jealous.

Penny stared at him for a few seconds until a smile formed on her face. She leaned in so only he could hear and said, "For the record, I don't think jealousy is a red flag."

That got his attention. And his dick's attention. "Oh yeah?"

"I think it's sort of...hot." She fanned her face for effect.

Now, he was sporting a full erection as he stood at the

table surrounded by people. He was also smiling ear-to-ear and was pretty sure nothing could take away his good mood.

Penny turned on her stool to face him fully, her knees pressing against his thigh. Her body-hugging clothing made his mouth water. She looked around the table before speaking. "What's going on with JT and Mya?"

He glanced around the table and saw what she saw. That neither JT nor Mya were there. "He says she irritates him and that's it. I don't believe it."

"Me neither. It's not her style to announce that she is going to hit on a guy. She just does it. I feel like she did it on purpose."

"Why would she want to annoy JT?" he asked.

Penny's eyes widened, and her mouth formed an O. "She likes him too."

He had the same thought at the same time. "That has to be it."

She clapped her hands. "This is great. I actually think they would be cute together."

Alec would keep his opinions on JT and Mya getting together to himself. He was fine with it, but the reality was that if they got together and then broke up, it would hinder his chances with Penny. He couldn't see beyond that at the moment.

"Guys," Annabelle and Ben stepped up behind them. "Want to go play pool? Gabe said the room is empty."

He was game. Anything that let him stare at Penny's ass was good with him.

He'd rather bend her over the table when they were alone, but this would work for now.

"I'm in," he said.

"Me too," Penny said.

Everyone grabbed their drinks and headed to the back room, where there was a pool table and a dart board. The bar as a whole wasn't too crowded, and from experience, it would stay that way. That left the pool table room open for them to enjoy. It was one of the reasons he enjoyed the place.

Currently, it was just the six of them, with both JT and Mya still out in the bar. "Who wants to go first?" he asked.

"I will," Penny said, raising her hand. "It's been a few years since I played, so whoever I go against needs to take it easy on me."

"I'll play you," Gabe said. "I also haven't played in a bit, so I know I'm rusty."

Alec stepped back, finding a stool against the wall. Ben sat down next to him while Annabelle and Jodi sat across the small room where there were more stools. His eyes were glued to Penny as she chose her cue.

"You might need to bring it down a notch," Ben said.

Alec didn't take his eyes off Penny but said, "No, I'm good."

Beside him, Ben laughed. "Okay. I guess I'll let you be then. Hey, did you know that JT's sister is coming to town next week?"

That had him turning his head to look at his friend. "Kennedy?" He knew Kennedy was JT's only sister, but he also knew that several years ago, Kennedy and Ben had dated. Much to JT's dismay.

"Yeah, Kennedy. She's coming for an interview."

"She might move here?" Alec wondered what that would do to Ben. He'd really liked Kennedy, and when she'd moved away, he'd been devastated. "Will that be weird?"

He shrugged. "I don't think so. It was like five years ago, and I don't have feelings for her anymore." He chose that moment to look across the room at Annabelle. Ben had it bad for her, no matter what he said.

Then, a question popped into his head. "How do you know she is coming here and might move back?"

Ben grimaced. "She texted me."

Somehow, Alec knew that was the case. Ben may be over Kennedy, but he had a feeling Kennedy wanted to start things back up. "You know that's a problem, right?"

"I know, I know." He nodded several times. "When she left, I was angry, but I'm not angry anymore. I thought what we had was love but it wasn't. I was dumb and naive and searching for someone to love." He hung his head, his fingers toying with the label of his beer. "I'm glad she left. I needed the kick in the ass that her leaving gave me."

Alec patted his friend on the back. "I've got your back if you need anything." He wasn't sure what else to say but he wanted Ben to know he had people in his corner. "The question is, how is JT going to take her being back in town?" JT and Kennedy were like oil and water. They didn't mesh. Kennedy tended to bulldoze people, and she was also a user. JT tried to be a good big brother, but at some point, he'd had to pull back, or she would have walked all over him.

"From what she said, she hasn't told him yet. I should probably warn him, huh?"

"I think so. And who knows, maybe she's changed." Even as he said the words, he knew they weren't true. Kennedy was who she was, and he doubted she had changed at all.

"YES!" Penny shouted as she made a shot in the corner pocket.

"Go, Pen!" Annabelle cheered her on from across the room.

Gabe spread his arms wide. "Hello, where is my cheering section?" He looked at Alec and Ben.

"Oh, our bad," Ben said. "We promise to do better." It was said with so much sarcasm that Gabe flipped him off, and Alec couldn't help but laugh.

Penny sauntered over toward him, turning and bending over the table. She looked back over her shoulder, catching his eye. "And here I thought you'd be rooting for me to win."

Her jeans were pulled tight over her ass, and it took everything inside him not to reach out and touch her. He looked from her ass to her face and then back to her ass. She saw everything he did and was smiling at his blatant appraisal of her ass. "Yeah, sorry, Gabe, but I'm with Penny."

"Traitor," Gabe said.

Penny gave him a wink before facing the table and lining up her shot. Again, she made it.

"I thought you said you were rusty," Gabe said, exasperation in his voice.

"I assumed I was." She shrugged. "But I guess I used to play so much that it's like riding a bike." She was chalking up her cue lazily like this was all no big deal to her.

"Exactly how much did you play?" Gabe asked.

Jodi spoke up. "Oh, did we forget to mention we were in a billiards club in college?"

Next to him, Ben laughed, but Gabe was not as amused. "Of fucking course you were."

Alec wasn't surprised and it was just one more thing to add to the list about Penny that made him like her. She was the whole package.

A package that he desperately wanted to unwrap and keep forever.

Chapter Twenty-Two

Penny

Her cheeks hurt from smiling.

That was all because of Alec.

He made her happy in a way she wasn't sure she'd ever been. He didn't judge her, didn't try to control her, and seemed to find it sexy that she could kick his ass at pool.

It would be hard to keep him at a distance after this.

And honestly, she wasn't sure she wanted to anymore. She liked him, and he liked her, so maybe they could have some sort of light relationship—a relationship where she wouldn't get her heart broken if he upped and left.

"What's that smile about?" Jodi asked, handing her a new drink.

"I'm just happy." It was the truth, so why lie?

"You do seem annoyingly happy. Is that because of Alec?"

She shrugged. "Maybe. I don't know." She looked to the

bar, where Alec animatedly told Mya and Annabelle a story. "I'm trying to figure out my next move here."

"That's easy. You take him home and fuck his brains out."

Penny busted out laughing. "I think I've got that part covered. It's what happens after our brains are mush that I'm unsure of."

Jodi put her hands up. "Fuck if I know."

Again, Penny laughed. "You and me both."

"Ladies," JT said, strolling up to them. "Would anyone like to dance?" He pointed to the dance floor, where several people were dancing to the pop music playing.

Penny hopped off her stool, set her drink on the table, and then grabbed Jodi's arm. "We both will." She liked dancing even though she was the worst at it, but she was just tipsy enough not to care.

Plus, there was no way she was turning down a chance to see what Alec would do when she was dancing.

The music was louder on the dance floor, and the three of them immediately joined in with the small crowd. They didn't try to talk because it was too loud. They just moved to the music along with everyone else.

When she looked at the bar, she saw Alec's eyes glued to her. They were dark with need, sending chills down her spine. His gaze was predatory, but she didn't hate it. She liked that he wanted her to the point of jealousy. It made her feel all tingly on the inside. It was weird because, before Alec, she would have said that jealousy was a red flag. Now, it felt more like a green flag.

Wanting to draw him to her, she changed her dance moves, making them more provocative. Or at least as provocative as she could. She didn't have a lot of skill or coordination, but she was willing to try.

And from the look on his face and the way he was now moving across the bar, directly toward her, she assumed it worked.

Before he reached her, Jodi whispered in her ear, "I think your plan worked." Penny turned her head, taking her eyes off Alec for just a second to look at her smirking friend.

Of course, she'd known what Penny was up to the whole time.

When she turned back around, Alec was right in front of her. He wasted no time wrapping an arm around her waist and leaning in. "Are you trying to get me to fuck you right here?"

She slowly slid her arms around his neck, loving the feel of being able to touch him. "Is that what you want to do?" she whispered in his ear.

His breath tickled her neck and ear as he said, "I always want to fuck you."

She smiled, unable to control it. She loved how open and honest he was with her. He never beat around the bush, and his dirty words turned her on in a way she'd never expected.

The music was still loud and pumping, but they stayed pressed together as they moved their bodies. She was lost to the feel of him, not caring about anything going on around them. His hands moved over every part of her, almost like he needed to touch her.

She knew how that felt because she needed to touch him. She wanted the freedom to dance with him and run her hands over his neck and through his hair. Why she ever thought having a rule where there was no touching was a good idea was beyond her.

Touching him was like a live wire to her heart.

She wasn't sure how long they danced or what was happening around them, but when Alec took her hand and guided her to a quiet corner, she knew exactly why.

They were on the same page.

He was about to speak when she closed the distance between them, pressing her lips against his.

Finally.

All night, all she'd wanted was to kiss him.

The kiss was possessive and powerful, and she never wanted it to end.

"Fuck, I love your mouth," he said against her lips as he tried to slow the kiss.

She was having none of that. She didn't care that just steps away, there were tons of people or that just hours ago, they had rules against this. None of it mattered.

Alec mattered.

He was all that mattered.

"Penny," he whispered her name in a way that made her panties even wetter. "We have to stop."

Her breathing was heavy as she pressed her forehead against him. "I know."

His hand squeezed her ass, helping to press her body even closer to his. "Believe me, I hate it as much as you, but if we keep kissing, I'm going to find a room in this place and fuck you in it, and I don't want that for us."

She closed her eyes, groaning because it sounded sort of divine. "Then take me home."

His hand came up, cupping her cheek. "Are you sure? Because I'm not sure I can keep doing whatever it was we were doing with the rules."

There was that honesty she loved so much. "I'm sure. I...

I still don't know...well, I don't know a lot, but I know I want you, and I'm sick of denying it."

His lips took hers in a hard, quick kiss. "Good, let's get out of here." Once again, he grabbed her hand as they headed through the bar.

She saw all their friends again at their table, and when they reached it, they stopped. "We're leaving," Alec said, his tone serious.

"Not shocking," Gabe said.

"Have fun!" Mya said. "Don't do anything I wouldn't do." She gave Penny a quick one-armed hug.

"Basically, the world is your oyster, then," Jodi said, shaking her head and smiling.

"Hey," Mya punched her in the arm.

Penny didn't hear or see the rest of the friendly argument because Alec once again guided them through the bar and out the door.

"Did you drive?" Alec asked.

She shook her head. "I took an Uber."

"Me too, which works since I don't think either of us should be driving right now."

He wasn't wrong. She'd had a lot to drink, which was one of the reasons she took Uber in the first place. He pulled out his phone, presumably ordering them a car.

"It'll be here in five minutes."

She leaned into his side, running her hand down his chest. "Do you have any suggestions on what we can do for five minutes?"

He grabbed her hand, stopping her movement. "I'm barely holding on here. You can't tease me."

"I thought we decided to throw the rules out. Which

means I can flirt all I want." She pulled her hand from his grip, continuing to caress his chest.

"Penny." Her name was a word of warning.

That only made her want to touch him more.

"Alec," she said in a drunken whisper, her hand going lower on his chest until her fingers came into contact with his belt.

He closed his eyes, groaning, his breath coming out heavy.

She stopped her hand where it was, not wanting to take this any further while they were in the parking lot. She wanted him alone.

And naked.

She stepped away from him, giving herself space to think. "Did you have fun tonight?"

"You know I did." He looked a little more relaxed now that she wasn't touching him, but his voice was rough with need.

She knew how he felt.

"What made you want to throw the rules out?" he asked.

Alcohol made her filterless, meaning he got the honest answer. "I was getting dressed and having a hard time doing so, might I say, because of the dumb rule about being sexy. You find everything I wear sexy. What was I supposed to do? Wear a garbage bag?"

"I can't help it if I find you sexy no matter what." He shrugged like it was just a forgone conclusion that he found her sexy.

"Anyway, at that moment, I decided that I hated the person I'd become since that last night in Mexico. I am usually confident and sure of myself. But somehow, I became this woman who had no idea what she wanted or who she was."

"Your confidence is one of the things I love about you."

His use of the word love had her blinking several times to make sure she wasn't dreaming. It also made her heart pound in her chest.

He could not have meant it the way she was thinking. It was just a word, and he probably didn't even know he had said it.

Thankfully, their ride pulled up, and she was able to settle the nerves that came with the use of that word.

In the backseat of the Uber, Alec sat close to her, his palm resting on her knee. They didn't speak, but the sexual tension that was radiating between them was volatile. She knew that as soon as they reached her apartment, it would be a mere minute before they were both naked, and he was inside her.

Which was fine with her.

More than fine.

When the driver stopped in front of her building, they both got out and, without a glance back, headed up the stairs to her apartment. She hurriedly typed in the code on the keypad while Alec pressed up against her back, swept her hair from her neck, and began kissing her skin.

She faltered, messing up the code, and had to type the numbers in a second time. This time, the door unlocked, and she pushed it open, turning in Alec's arms. He reached behind him, closing the door as their mouths met in a desperate kiss.

He continued to move them further into her living space until her legs hit the couch.

"You're wearing too many clothes." She started pulling at his shirt.

"So are you." Together, they undressed at the speed of light, their hands and lips touching bare skin whenever they could.

When they were both naked, he flipped her around, pushing her down until she was bent over the arm of the couch, and her ass was in the air. "I need you like this the first time." She heard the crinkle of the condom wrapper, and when she turned her head to look over her shoulder, she saw him rolling it down his cock.

He locked eyes with her as his hand delved between her legs. "You're so fucking wet."

"I don't need any foreplay. Just fuck me." That was the absolute truth. She'd been thinking about him since he'd walked out the door days ago, and she couldn't wait a second longer.

The whole night had been a version of foreplay.

Which was why she was so wet and ready.

She felt his dick nudge her opening, and then his hands grabbed her hips, his fingers digging into the skin as he entered her in one hard thrust.

"Fuck!" he roared out.

She moaned at how good he felt, pushing her ass back against him. "Harder." She gave him one last look over her shoulder, seeing the heat in his eyes.

He took her at her word and began fucking her in long, hard strokes. She held onto the couch, moaning and speaking incoherent words as his cock worked her pussy. When he slapped her ass, she begged for more, which he seemed to have no problem giving her.

After three or four more slaps—she lost count—he

dipped his fingers between her legs and strummed her clit as he continued to pound into her. It only took a few strokes of his fingers against her clit to have her coming.

"Oh shit, oh shit," she chanted, her body on fire as he continued to fuck her through her orgasm.

"Oh yeah, squeeze my cock with that pussy." His words were dirty but perfect, and just what she liked.

He grunted as he pounded into her body a few more times, and when he came, he pressed inside her so deep that she thought she might come again. He held himself inside her as he slumped over her, kissing her shoulder and neck.

"Fuck, I've missed you." His whispered words, choppy from being out of breath, made her happy.

His willingness to be open and honest was sexy.

"If you let me up, we can do it again. This time in a bed."

He laughed, giving her shoulder one last lingering kiss before standing up and pulling out of her body. She missed the connection instantly but knew she'd have it again.

She'd been a fool the last week, but no longer. Sex with Alec was too good to go back to pretending it wasn't. She wasn't going to bring it up yet, but later, she'd see what he thought about making this a more permanent thing.

Not a relationship because she wasn't sure that was something she was ready for, but she also wasn't willing to share him with other people. If they were going to sleep together, it had to be exclusive.

"Come on." She swatted his ass as she walked past him. "I've got days of sex to make up for." She looked over her shoulder to see him follow her in all his naked glory.

"You won't hear me complain." He caught up to her just as they reached her bedroom, spinning her around and taking her mouth in a punishing kiss. "Get on the bed and spread your legs."

She shivered at what his words promised. His head between her legs was a celestial experience.

One she never wanted to end.

Chapter Twenty-Three

Alec

He should be exhausted and worn out, but all he could think about as he sat on Penny's bed, eating pizza with her by his side, was that he wanted her again.

He wasn't even sure how his dick could still get hard.

They'd had sex three times in two hours. That was three orgasms for him and six for her, and yet, his body and brain knew that as soon as they finished eating, he'd be all over her again.

"Why is pizza so good after you've been drinking?" Penny said around a mouthful of pizza.

Even talking while eating was sexy when she did it.

"It's gotta be the grease," he said, taking a giant bite of his own slice.

"I think you're right." She finished off the last of her slice before wiping her mouth and hands with a napkin. "As good as that was, you know what will be better? Sleep." She scooted down until her head was on the pillow, turning to look at him. "Someone wore me out."

He laughed as he finished his slice of pizza. Then, he took the box and set it on the table beside the bed. "I think you're misremembering it." He laid down, facing her and pulling her against him.

Their faces were mere inches apart. He looked into her eyes, using his hand to push the hair from her face. "Do you want me to go?"

Her eyes widened. "No. Stay."

"If I stay, I'm not sure I can promise I won't wake you up more than once throughout the night." It was the truth. He'd been without her for what felt like too long, and if he was near her, he wanted to touch her.

She ran her hand up and down his side. "I'm counting on it." She leaned in and kissed him gently.

That gentle kiss led to them kissing for minutes. His hands explored her body slowly and sensually as hers did the same. When the tension became too much, Alec dipped his hand between her legs, slowly and efficiently stroking her clit.

His motions stayed easy, slowly bringing her to the brink before backing off. She moaned into his mouth as her body pressed harder against his hand for more friction. The sounds she made were so intoxicating and had his dick leaking with need.

But this was for her.

He would and could forgo pleasure if it meant making her happy.

Her pussy was drenched, his fingers having trouble staying on her clit. Saying fuck it, he dipped them lower, pressing inside her.

"Oh yes," she moaned. "Please."

"I love your tight pussy and want you to come all over my hand." His brain-to-mouth filter was gone whenever he was with her. But she seemed to love the dirty things he said to her.

"Make me come," she murmured, her eyes glued to his, letting him know this was precisely what she wanted.

He grabbed her leg, hooking it over his hip for better access. She moaned when his fingers penetrated at a different angle, somehow going even deeper. He pressed his forehead against hers, still holding her gaze.

With their gazes locked, it was like a binding of two souls as she came, her body shaking and drenching his hand.

At that moment, seeing her trust in him, he knew what he felt for her was love.

Weirdly, he was perfectly content with that recognition.

"It's like you know my body better than I do," she said, rolling onto her back but keeping her eyes on him. "I'm not sure how I feel about that."

He chuckled. "Making you come is like a religious experience. You don't hold back, and I fucking love it."

He watched as she closed her eyes, breathing deeply. Within minutes, she was asleep while he was still wide awake after his revelation that he loved her. Making sure not to jostle her, he got up from the bed to check the door and turn off the lights. When that was done, he found both their phones, plugging them in to make sure they were charged before re-joining her in bed.

He pulled the covers up over them and then wrapped his body around hers. She murmured his name, pushing her body back against his in her sleep.

That made him smile.

She may not be great at admitting it when she was awake, but when she was asleep, her body sought him out.

That was a start.

* * *

He woke up when the bed shifted, and when he opened his eyes, he found Penny moving between his legs.

"Hey," his voice was raspy from sleep.

"Oh damn." She gave him a sexy smile. "I was hoping to wake you up with your dick in my mouth." She gripped his cock in her hand, stroking it up and down.

His body went from sleep to fully awake in a matter of seconds. "I think this is just as good. Now I can watch." He crossed his arms under his head, ready to completely give in to this blow job.

She bit her bottom lip, her eyes filled with heat. "Keep your hands there," she said as she lowered her body down, her mouth directly over his dick.

Was it really only weeks ago that he thought blowjobs were pointless? It seemed ridiculous now.

He could feel the heat from her breath as she continued to stroke him up and down. He waited with bated breath for her to put her mouth on him. The wait was tortuous. He itched to reach down and press against her head so she'd finally take him in her mouth, but he held back. This was her show, and he would give her all the control.

Even if it killed him.

Just when he thought he couldn't take it anymore, she licked up the underside of his shaft once before sliding her mouth down over him.

"Fuck yeah," he swore. Her mouth was hot and wet and

fucking perfect. Penny had changed his stance on blow jobs with that perfect mouth.

Now, he craved them.

But only from her.

She worked him over like an expert and did so effortlessly. He reveled in the way her head bobbed up and down and how, every few strokes, she'd flick her gaze to his. He groaned loudly, trying his damndest to hold back. He didn't want it to end.

He wanted it to go on and on and on until the end of forever.

That option wasn't viable, especially when she hummed around his dick and toyed with his balls.

"Oh fuck, I'm gonna come." He glued his eyes to where they were connected and watched as she sucked him deeper one last time. Holding back wasn't an option, and he came in an eruption down her throat.

She didn't miss a drop and when she sat back and licked her lips, he had to close his eyes before he confessed his love right then and there.

"Good morning," she said, moving back up the bed to lie beside him.

"It sure as fuck was." He tucked her into his side, running his fingers up and down her arm.

They lay there like that for a few minutes, the silence somehow comfortable.

"Should we talk?" she spoke first, breaking him out of his blowjob-induced haze.

"Probably." He knew they needed to, but he was scared on two fronts. One, that he would declare his love at the wrong time, and two, that she would end this once again.

Even worse, what if he told her he loved her, and that

made her end it?

It was a double-edged sword if there ever was one.

She sat up, pulling the covers up to hold against her naked chest. He sat, too, figuring it would be better that way.

"So it's obvious that we can't stay away from each other," she started with a smirk on her face.

"Yeah, I'd say that's a fact." It was undisputed. If she was near, he was drawn to her like a magnet.

"And we both like the sex."

"Like is a little understated, but go on."

She laughed. "I'm thinking maybe we make this a normal thing."

That had his happy mood halting. "Huh?"

She gestured between them, "Maybe we can meet up once or twice a week and do this."

He furrowed his brow. "Wait, you just want to have sex?"

"Well, yeah. Don't you?" The way she said it, so calm and easy, made him angry.

"No. Fuck no." He threw the covers off, standing up and looking around for what he wasn't sure.

"Why are you getting mad?"

She had no clue. She fucking had no clue. Here he was full-on in love with her, and she was talking about sex. Just fucking sex.

"Because I thought we were on the same page after last night but I guess I was wrong." He stomped out of the room, going in search of his clothes which were in a pile on her couch where he'd placed them after he'd fucked her brains out.

Fucking. That's all this was to her.

"Are you leaving?" He looked up to see that she'd pulled

on a t-shirt before following him into the living room.

Thank god because her naked body would make him agree to anything.

"No." He pulled his pants on. "Or maybe. I don't know. I just needed to be dressed." He calmed his voice, not liking how he was reacting.

"I thought we were on the same page here," she said, her head tilted to the side, confusion in her eyes.

"I thought so too. Seems like we were both wrong."

She took a step toward him but he put up a hand to stop her. "I need you to stay a few feet back. When you touch me, I lose all thought."

"Is that a bad thing?"

"Normally no, but if all you want is sex, I think it might be." Even saying the words made him want to vomit. Was he really going to give all this up, give her up just because she only wanted sex?

"I don't think I have more to give than that," she said almost sadly.

Seeing her sad broke his heart. But at the same time, his was breaking too. He had no clue what to do, or what was right or wrong, but he had to protect himself.

"Maybe we had it right the first time," he said.

"What does that mean?"

"No contact. Not friends, not sex, just...nothing." Saying the words was like taking a knife and chiseling his heart out of his chest. But he couldn't do this halfway shit anymore.

"I see." She dropped her head, looking down at her feet. "If that's what you want, then I guess I have to agree."

He wanted to argue, to tell her to fight for them, for him. But if she didn't want that, want him, he had to let it go. Let her go.

"It's not what I want but I think it's what you want." He grabbed his shirt from the couch and then slipped on his shoes.

When he was fully dressed, he looked at her and, in a last-minute decision, went to her and pulled her into his arms. She hesitated only a second before wrapping her arms around him. He kissed the top of her head, letting himself relish in the feel of her against him one last time.

"I'll miss you," he murmured against her hair more for himself, but he knew she could hear him.

When he pulled back, because it was that or stay and beg her to love him, he nodded and then turned to the door. Only then did he remember he'd put his phone by the bed. "Uh, my phone is in your room."

She looked confused.

"Last night, after you fell asleep, I locked up, turned the lights off, and grabbed both our phones to charge them." He wasn't sure why he was explaining what he did, maybe just to have something to say to make things less awkward.

"I'll get it," she said, her voice barely audible.

Before he could object, she walked away and, only seconds later, returned with his phone.

She held it out for him to take, their fingers brushing. "Thank you." He swallowed the lump that had formed in his throat. "I guess I'll see you around."

The finality of those words didn't hit him until he was outside her door and in the parking lot.

He was walking away from the woman he loved. It hurt. Badly. But he couldn't continue to love her if she didn't love him.

This was how it had to be.

Chapter Twenty-Four

Penny

She wasn't sure how long she stood in her living room staring at the door. When she finally moved, it was to fall down on the couch.

Even as she told herself that she wasn't going to cry, tears streamed down her face.

They'd had the perfect night together. She'd thought everything was good. Then he'd gone and blown it all apart.

And she couldn't figure out why.

He'd said more than once that if all she wanted was sex, then he was out. What did that mean? He'd never once said what he wanted or how he felt.

She wasn't a fucking mind reader.

It didn't matter, at least not anymore, because he'd left. Instead of staying and talking, he'd fucking left.

Again.

That was twice that he'd left her and twice that he'd broken her heart.

She was done. Finished.

Wiping the tears from her eyes, she was determined to forget that Alec ever existed.

Easier said than done, she suspected.

Needing to stay busy and keep her mind off him, she cleaned in a frenzy. Scrubbing counters and floors, washing all her bedding, and rearranging her bathroom cabinet. Hours later, she slid to the floor in her bathroom, pulling her knees to her chest as she stared at the wall.

She was exhausted both physically and emotionally. Cleaning hadn't really helped keep her mind from Alec. It had only pushed him aside for a short period of time. He was back, invading every part of her mind and body. She remembered all the fun they'd had and how sweet and caring he was.

He'd gotten out of bed and made sure her door was locked and the lights were out. Then he'd plugged in her phone. What kind of person did that?

A good one.

That's what he was. A good guy.

And if that was the case, what the fuck was she doing? Why had she told him she only wanted sex?

But it didn't matter. It couldn't matter. He'd left. Again. He didn't want to be with her.

Clueless about what to think or do, she pulled her phone from her pocket and sent an SOS to her friends.

Penny:
I need to talk.

The responses were immediate.

Annabella:
On the way!
Jodi:
I'm actually close by, be there in a few.
Mya:
Getting in my car now.

She dropped her phone, closing her eyes. Thank god she had her friends. She wasn't sure what she would do without them.

Less than ten minutes later, she heard voices and knew one of them had arrived. They all had the code to her door and could come and go as they pleased. When both Annabelle and Jodi appeared in the doorway of her bathroom, the tears that she thought she'd shoved deep down inside came spilling out.

"Oh, babe." Annabelle stepped into the small bathroom, sat down beside her, and wrapped her arm around her.

"What happened?" Jodi said, joining them on the floor and sitting across from them.

The tiny bathroom was cramped with three of them, but their willingness to sit with her in the small space proved how special they were.

"He left. He just left." Saying the words was like reliving it all over again.

Annabelle hugged her tighter. "Want me to go kill him for you?"

They made her laugh through her tears.

"Tell us what happened," Jodi said. "Because I saw you two together last night, and that man likes you."

She shook her head as tears fell. "We had a great night

together." She went on to tell them about the night and their conversation that morning when he got angry and left.

"Oh, Pen," Jodi said. "I love you, but you are an idiot."

"An adorable, lovable idiot," Annabelle added.

"What are you talking about?"

"He wanted more," Jodi said.

She shook her head repeatedly. "No, he didn't."

"Yes, he did." They all looked to the doorway, where Mya had suddenly appeared. "Does, I should say." Like the rest of them, she sat down. "It's the only explanation for how angry he was."

"Agree," Annabelle said. "Is he also an idiot for not spelling it out to you? Definitely. But my guess is that just like you, he was scared."

She closed her eyes, trying to remember everything about their conversation. The way he looked, the way he sounded, but all she saw was his anger. "I think you guys are wrong."

"Babe," Mya said, "look at me. Why was he angry? Can you explain that?"

Penny shook her head because she didn't know then, nor did she know now.

"He was angry because you said you just wanted to be friends who had sex here and there, and he wanted more," Mya said.

She tried to take in what Mya was saying, but it just didn't compute in her brain.

"I'm with Mya," Jodi said. "He wanted more. A relationship."

That word...relationship...made her itchy. She wanted that with him but was afraid he didn't. That was why she'd suggested they just have sex. But if he wanted a relationship, that changed things.

"Do you guys really think that?"

"YES!" they all three said at the same time.

She dropped her head into her hands. "Shit, I think I fucked up." She looked up. "I was so afraid of getting hurt if he didn't want more with me that I pushed him away."

"You've never been afraid before," Annabelle said. "Why is this different?"

It was time to be truthful with herself and her friends. "Because he's different. I was never in love with any of them. At least not this kind of love. It was stupid love. Love that I thought would last but obviously never did. Alec is the real thing, and it scares me."

When she looked around at her friends, they were all smiling from ear to ear.

"So what are you going to do about it?" Jodi asked.

Wasn't that the million-dollar question? "I guess I'm going to have to talk to him." The pit that formed in her stomach at the thought of him rejecting her was massive.

"What are you waiting for?" Mya said.

"What?" she looked around. "You want me to do it now?"

"YES!" they screamed.

She took a couple of deep breaths. "But what if..."

"No," Jodi said definitively. "No what-ifs. You love him, and you need to tell him that."

Annabelle rubbed her back. "He won't reject you."

"I'll drive," Mya jumped up.

Uncertainty swirled throughout her mind. So many things could go wrong with just showing up at his house and telling him how she felt.

"Stop stalling," Jodi said. "If you want him, want this, then you need to go now. You can't let it get worse."

She stood up, looking around the small room at her friends. "I don't know what I'd do without you guys."

"Yeah, yeah, yeah," Annabelle said. "We love you too, now go get your man." She shoved Penny out of the bathroom.

"I need to change first." She looked down at the black sweatpants and old t-shirt she was wearing.

"There's no time," Mya said. "Plus, he's made it very obvious that it's not your clothes he likes."

Mya made a good point. He never seemed to care what she was wearing and his stupid rule about dressing sexy had been hard to follow because he seemingly found everything she wore sexy.

She was a fucking idiot.

He was telling her with his words and actions that he liked her and she'd been oblivious, only worrying about herself.

She'd never put him first but that was about to change.

He deserved to be her first thought each morning and last thought each night.

The trepidation she'd had only moments ago about going to see him was gone and now she needed to see him. Needed him to know that she loved him and she would always put him first.

"Let's go," she demanded, already moving through her apartment toward her door.

Then, just as she grabbed the doorknob, there was an almost frantic pounding on her door.

She looked at her friends, who were all there. There was only one person who could be on the other side.

"It's him," Jodi said, whispering "It has to be."

Her heartbeat sped up. He'd come back.

"Open it," Mya said.

Without a second of hesitation, she pulled the door open and sure enough, there he stood, rumpled and sexy, his eyes wild with emotion.

Her heart melted at his feet into a puddle of love.

Chapter Twenty-Five

Alec

He'd gone home, doing his best to forget Penny ever existed.

Only it wasn't as easy as it sounded.

She was all he thought about and all he wanted.

Which was how he'd ended up at her door, ready to demand that she love him.

A ridiculous demand, he was well aware, but he also wasn't sure he could lose her. She was who he wanted to spend his life with. It didn't matter that they'd only known each other a short amount of time.

He'd do whatever it took to keep her in his life. If that meant only sex, while she figured out what she wanted, he'd do it.

After pounding on her door several times, it finally opened, the woman he loved staring back at him.

Her eyes were puffy and her face was red with splotches from her obvious crying. He hated that he'd made her cry.

"We're out of here." He looked up to see Mya, Jodi and Annabelle standing behind Penny.

"If you need us, call," Jodi said.

All three of them gave him a look of encouragement as they passed him.

It was too hard to look at her and not tell her how he felt any longer.

They spoke at the same time.

"Penny."

"Alec."

"Just let me get this out and then you can kick me out," he said.

"You don't need to and I'm not going to kick you out." She reached out, grabbing his hand and pulling him into her apartment before shutting the door. "I fucked up."

That was not what he'd expected. He'd thought for sure that he'd have to beg for her forgiveness. "What are you talking about?"

She didn't let go of his hand, instead bringing it to her chest, cradling it there like it was precious. "I was so afraid of getting my heart broken that I didn't see what was right in front of my face. You. You were right there, showing me at every turn that you were all in."

Her words held so much emotion, giving him so much hope. He cupped her cheek, running his thumb gently over her red skin. "Hiding what I felt for you was never something I wanted to do."

Her eyes filled with tears. "I know that now and when I look back, everything you did and said was real and true. I'm the one who was so scared of letting you love me and loving you back that I tried to keep it simple."

"And now?" He was so hopeful at her words. She'd basically just admitted to loving him.

She laughed. "I'm still scared but not of how I feel about you."

"And how do you feel?" He gave her a devilish smile, closing the distance between them until they were as close as could be without kissing.

She bit down on her bottom lip. "It's like that day you taught me to surf. It was scary and intimidating at first. But then you told me to just stop thinking and do it. So that's what I'm doing. I'm not going to think about anything but loving you."

He cupped her other cheek, pressing his forehead against hers." I love you. So fucking much." He pressed his lips against hers, kissing her fiercely. When they were both breathless from the kiss, he pulled back, smiling. "I can't believe you just used surfing as a reference."

She smiled brightly, the tears she'd recently shed glimmering in her eyes. "That day just kept coming back to me when I thought about losing you. You believed in me from the start but what I remembered most was that you said we were a lot alike."

He grabbed her around the waist pulling her down onto the couch with him, her falling onto his lap. It felt so good to have her back in his arms. "What's so special about that? I think we are alike."

She stroked her hand down his cheek. "I just kept thinking that if we were so alike then maybe you were also unable to say what you were feeling to me. That thought, along with my friends, kicked me in the ass."

"So many times, I wanted to tell you how I felt, but I was a coward." He took a deep breath. "When I got to my house this morning, all I could think was that I was an idiot for leaving when all I'd wanted to do was stay and tell you that I loved you."

"What took you so long to come back?"

That was the question he'd been asking himself since he left. "I think it was pride. I was so focused on not getting my heart broken that I failed to realize it was already broken if I didn't have you in my life. When I finally realized that, I knew I had to see you immediately."

"I was coming to you too, you know," she said. "I'd like that to be noted." She tilted her head, smiling with humor.

He laughed. "I'll be sure to make note of it in the official transcript."

They giggled together which turned into them kissing for long minutes. His hands journeyed down her body, wanting to touch every part of her. Her hands were tangled in his hair, tugging gently to bring them even closer together.

"Alec, make love to me," she murmured as he kissed her neck.

Make love.

Those words from her mouth were music to his ears. She loved him, and from now on, when they were together, they'd always be making love, even if they were fucking.

There was something sort of poetic about that.

Epilogue

Penny

Being in love was wild.

Sure, it had only been four days since she and Alec had made up and admitted their love for each other, but those four days had been amazing.

They texted during work, met up for lunch, and spent their nights together. He'd stayed at her apartment at first, but then she realized it was silly to be at her place when he had a whole house.

A house she loved.

The first time time he'd taken her there, she'd been amazed at how big it was for a single guy. He'd explained that his grandparents had left him some money when they passed away and he'd used it to purchase the house. Then over the last ten years, together with his dad and brother, they'd remodeled most of it.

Penny loved everything about it. The kitchen was huge

and the primary bedroom had an attached bath that was practically the size of her whole apartment.

That was an exaggeration, but still, it was huge.

Oh, and his bed was so large, they could sleep without touching. Alec swore that was the worst part and he teased that he was going to order a smaller bed so she'd be forced to sleep snuggled up against him.

Tonight, her friends were coming by for a girls' night while Alec was playing basketball with his friends. She'd planned to have the gathering at her apartment since it was her turn to host, but Alec had insisted she have it at his place.

She was just setting out a platter of munchies when the door opened and Mya walked in with Annabelle and Jodi behind her.

"Knock much?" Penny asked.

Mya scoffed. "I don't knock at your apartment. Why do I have to knock here?"

"I told her to knock," Jodi said. "God forbid you and Alec were naked on the couch. That is not something I need to see."

"We knew he wasn't here," Annabelle said, snatching a piece of cheese off the platter and then plopping down on the couch.

"I made margaritas, if you want one," Penny told them. "Or I have wine."

"Margaritas," they said in unison.

Penny poured four glasses and handed one to each of them before sitting down. "Catch me up on everything." She'd been cocooned in her love bubble with Alec for days and hadn't paid much attention to anything else.

"Oh no," Annabelle said. "Don't even think about ignoring the elephant in the room. You first."

Penny laughed. "You guys know everything there is to know. I fucked up, he fucked up and now we are together."

"While all of that may be true, you owe us more," Mya said. "We sat on your bathroom floor and consoled you when you thought it was over. We deserve details."

"Oh my god, you're insane." Penny took a big sip of her margarita.

"Not insane," Jodi said, "just curious."

She set her glass on the table in front of her. "Things are great. Really great."

"Boring," Mya said. "Give us more."

"What do you want me to say?" she asked with a laugh. "That the sex is incredible? You knew that already."

"Are you living here?" Jodi asked.

"No," she shook her head, a little shocked by the question. "It's been a week."

"Really, it's been like three," Annabelle said. "And you guys are together every night."

"We like to sleep together. And by sleep, I mean actually sleep."

"Do you think you'll move in?" Mya asked.

The conversation made her antsy. She wanted a future with Alec and they'd talked about it a lot, but it was too early to be talking about living together. "I don't know. I mean, I'm sure eventually we will live together."

"Big step," Jodi said. "You've never lived with a guy."

"Neither have you," she was quick to reply.

"None of us have," Annabelle said.

"Hey, I lived with my brother right after college," Mya said.

"That doesn't count," Penny said.

"Remember the parade of girls he'd bring home nightly?"

Annabelle asked, giggling. "I love your brother, but I will never understand how he got so many girls."

Penny completely understood what Annabelle was saying. They all did. Mya's brother was not exactly what you'd call good looking. But the guy could get almost any woman.

"God, I hated living with him," Mya said. "I had to wear noise canceling headphones every night because I never knew what I'd hear if I didn't. And the amount of women I saw do the walk of shame from his bedroom was insane."

They fell into a fit of laughter and it pretty much stayed like that until the guys came walking in through the kitchen from the garage.

Her eyes went immediately to Alec.

"Sounds like you're having fun," he said as he made his way to her, bending down and giving her a long kiss.

"None of that!" Mya threw a pillow at them.

Penny looked up at him, her smile growing bigger. "We are. How was basketball?"

JT flopped down on the couch saying, "We kicked ass."

"Dude you're sitting on my couch all sweaty," Alec said. "We've talked about this."

"You've talked," Ben said, joining JT on the couch, "we've refused to listen."

Alec shook his head, making Penny laugh. "One beer and then you assholes are out of here," Alec said.

"I'll help." Penny jumped up from her chair, following Alec into the kitchen.

She didn't make it far before he had her pushed up against the wall, hiding them from view. "Fuck, I missed you." He kissed her neck as he pressed his body against hers.

Her hands immediately went to his head, gripping his

hair. "I missed you too." She pulled on his hair, wanting his mouth on hers. This kiss was electric after a full day apart.

Would it always be this way?

She hoped so.

"Let's kick our friends out," he murmured against her lips.

She chuckled. "Good luck with that."

He sighed, letting his forehead lean against hers. "I like you in my house."

She searched his eyes, wondering if his words hid another meaning. But then she remembered that they'd promised to always be honest and say what was on their minds. "I like being in your house." She swallowed the lump of uncertainty. "You know, my lease is up in two months." Saying the words was freeing and yet, so freaking scary.

He didn't blink and his expression didn't change.

She had no clue what he was thinking.

Until he spoke.

"That's great and all, but I'm not sleeping apart from you for two months."

A smile formed on her lips. She should have known that he'd say something like that. "I need more than that."

He gave her a quick, hard kiss. "I was planning to ask you to move in here in a few weeks." He shrugged. "I like you in my space."

"I like being in your space." She snaked her hand between their bodies, gripping his hard cock through his basketball shorts. "Especially when I get treats like this."

He groaned. "I fucking love you. So much."

She squeezed him one more time before letting go. "Get your friend their drinks so they can drink them and get the hell out of here. Then I will show you just how much I love you."

He kissed her again, this time slow and seductively. "Or we can just lock ourselves in our room and say fuck it."

Our room.

He was already calling it theirs.

Her heart flipped in her chest and she somehow fell even more in love with him.

Just like that day in the ocean when he taught her to surf, she decided to just do instead of thinking. With a gleam in her eye, she grabbed his hand, pulling him out of the kitchen and through the living room. "Party's over!" she yelled not even looking at their friends.

Behind her, Alec laughed, grabbing her around the waist and practically carrying her into the bedroom.

She had no doubt that she was going to love this man for the rest of her life.

Milton Keynes UK
Ingram Content Group UK Ltd.
UKHW010020030424
440481UK00001B/65

9 798224 912247